THE FAITHLESS

THE FAITHLESS

A POLITICAL THRILLER

BY

ALLAN AIRISH

MARGINAL ENTERTAINMENT VALUE BOOKS

For Dad

"A nation which asks nothing of its government but the maintenance of order is already a slave at heart—the slave of its own well-being, awaiting but the hand that will bind it.

"By such a nation the despotism of faction is not less to be dreaded than the despotism of an individual. When the bulk of the community is engrossed by private concerns, the smallest parties need not despair of getting the upper hand in public affairs. At such times it is not rare to see upon the great stage of the world, as we see at our theatres, a multitude represented by a few players, who alone speak in the name of an absent or inattentive crowd: they alone are in action whilst all are stationary; they regulate everything by their own caprice; they change the laws, and tyrannize at will over the manners of the country; and then men wonder to see into how small a number of weak and worthless hands a great people may fall."

—Alexis de Tocqueville, *Democracy in America* (1840)

1

THE VOICE on the other end of the phone was raspy with grief and exhausted tears: "Come home, Jack. It's time."

Jack Patton had known for months that the call was coming, but still wasn't ready for what it meant. He stared numbly at his computer screen; a whimsical illustration of a polar bear stared back—part of a logo he was designing for a local air-conditioning company. He shut it down without saving and grabbed his shoulder bag as he headed for the door.

"Marlene, I'm gonna be out of pocket for a while," he said to a bored young receptionist as he passed. "Tell Silas I'll call him about the Polar Air job. And try not to let anyone burn the place to the ground while I'm gone."

"Wait, what?" she asked, looking as if she'd just been shaken awake. "Where are you going?"

"Home," he said. "I mean, Nobles. Little town west of here."

"When are you coming back?" she asked as Jack walked off.

"That depends."

"On?"

"On how long it takes my dad to die," he called back, then disappeared out the door.

*   *   *

Nobles was only an hour from Austin, but as far as Jack was concerned, it was a world removed. He hadn't talked to his immediate family for months; they were pretty much exactly as he left them twenty years before, biding time in a town that offered no opportunities beyond just getting by. On the increasingly rare occasions that he came back to visit, it seemed to him that the town itself was a reflection of his father's condition, or vice versa.

As the old man slowly wasted away, so too did the last remnants of prosperity in the once-thriving business square around City Hall. The last time he came out, he found Leyendecker's Hardware vacant along the southern promenade—the fading paint on the side still proclaiming "Since 1923"—like a front tooth extracted from a diseased mouth. The only business that still seemed to thrive on the square was a medical supply store, whose window display proclaimed, "Diabetic Shoes are IN!"

As Jack pulled into the driveway of his childhood home, overgrown vines of Confederate jasmine whispered against his doors on either side. He felt a stab of guilt. Obviously his dad hadn't been able to keep the place up in his condition, and Vera Lynn had been too busy taking care of dad. He made a mental note to trim the vines before he left.

Other than the neglect in the yard, the house hadn't changed at all. It was like a time capsule from Jack's youth. The same ceramic pig knickknacks lined the porch rail, the same ostentatious (and always dusty) chandelier hung in the foyer... even the cat that greeted him at the door—a gray long-hair—looked like the cat he grew up with. It occurred to Jack that the two were probably related, since his father had never been keen on spaying or neutering. "What do you mean, 'get the cat fixed'?" his father used to say. "That cat ain't broke."

Jack's older sister was in the kitchen, hands filled with trays of deviled eggs. When she spotted him, she barely registered a hitch in her step. "Look who's back," she said.

"Good to see you too, Vera Lynn," he said.

His father's room was dim, as he preferred it. Like the rest of the house, the decor had remained the same. Most important was the wall above the dresser, where his most prized accomplishments were documented: his law degree, framed in ornate mahogany; a campaign button and newspaper article from the year he was first elected judge; and a picture of him and his only son standing next to President Reagan. On top of the dresser rested his well-worn gavel, and a satin-lined oak box containing a pen that he valued more highly than anything else.

"Dad, Jack's here," Vera Lynn said.

The old man opened his yellowed eyes and, slowly, they fixed on Jack. He lifted a dry, withered hand, and Jack took it between his own.

"My boy," the old man said.

Jack wanted to say something back—so many things, in fact, that his head was swimming—but as he opened his mouth, his throat pinched tight and his eyes blurred with tears. He squeezed his father's hand harder, hoping the message got through by sheer force.

The old man shifted his head toward the wall above the dresser. "You remember that?" he asked.

Jack knew that he was talking about the picture with President Reagan. He nodded his head vigorously. Jack had been just ten years old at the time; he was thrilled at the thought of a trip to Washington, D.C. with his dad, just the two of them. But instead of going to museums and monuments, they spent most of their time meeting with stodgy old men in suits that all smelled of the same aftershave. The only exciting part was the visit to the White House, where the picture was taken. While they were waiting to meet the president, his father asked him, "Do you know how many votes it takes to be elected President of the United States?"

Jack shrugged. At ten, he had no grasp of large numbers, but he knew that adults from all around the country had made a big deal about voting the previous November. "I dunno. A million billion."

His father chuckled. "Two hundred and seventy," he said. "That's all the votes you need to become president, as long as it's the right ones. And this time, *I* was one of those votes."

At the time, Jack had suspected that his father was joking. After all, he knew there were a hundred and fifty kids in his grade at school back home, and each one of them had two parents (except for Lynn Halsey, whose dad got drunk and fell out of his fishing boat the summer before). So there were at least three hundred adults in town, and all of them could vote. How could the President of the United States be elected by less people than there were in one small town? It just seemed like a setup for a hokey punch line that never came. Even after his father explained the electoral college process in detail, Jack remained skeptical until he heard the same story in history class two years later.

Staring at the picture on the wall, his father said weakly, "I didn't want you to be like me." He drew a ragged breath. "I just wanted you to be... part of something."

Jack wanted to get it all out while he still had time. He wanted to apologize for switching majors during his sophomore year, from pre-law to art. He wanted to explain that he tried, he really did, but his heart and talents just didn't match his father's ambitions. He also wanted to convince his father that he was successful in his own way; he owned his own business, he was a member of the Austin Chamber of Commerce. He wanted to say all of this, but none of the words came.

He wasn't sure how long he stood there, squeezing his father's hand. Finally, Vera Lynn stepped forward and took Jack firmly by the shoulder. "Uncle Travis would like some time with Daddy," she said, and ushered Jack from the room. Standing in the kitchen amid a growing group of relatives and friends, he felt like just one in a long line of visitors. That may have been Vera Lynn's intention; Jack knew that she had devoted much of her time and energy to caring for their father over the past few years. Meanwhile, Jack—just an hour's drive away—might just as well have lived across the country for all the help he was.

After Uncle Travis's visit, it was Mayor Utley's turn, then the Showalters, who had lived down the street for forty years. After just a couple of minutes the Showalters hurried out of the room, sobbing and clutching each other tightly. Vera Lynn appeared in the doorway, her face buried in her trembling hands.

He was gone.

2

THE HOUSE on Shelby Lane wasn't exactly a quick trip from Washington, D.C. It took two hours on a good day, heading east on U.S. Route 50 through Annapolis, over the hump of the monstrous Chesapeake Bay Bridge that binds urban western Maryland to its rural eastern counterpart. It was fall, and the undulating lowlands of the Delmarva Peninsula were ablaze with orange and gold.

As the man in the black sedan continued east across the Delaware border, traffic thinned enough for him to make sure he wasn't being followed. He continued past the poultry farms along Vernon Road (he always made sure to roll his windows up in advance) until he finally reached Harrington. Instead of heading straight to the house, he went to Rustic Spoon on Commerce Street and ordered some beef and dumplings to go. It was both an added precaution and his first real chance to eat since leaving D.C.

Back in his sedan, he headed to Shelby Lane. The house was typical suburban 1960s construction, single story brick with an unusual U-shaped driveway that circled all the way around the back side instead of just the front. Once he pulled in, his car was invisible from the main road; that was what had sold him on the place.

From the outside, the house appeared empty, but once he unlocked the deadbolt and swung the door open, he was enveloped in the comforting buzz of people at work. A freckled blonde swiveled in her chair as he entered. "Mister Langhorne," she said. "We've got a problem." She held out a packet of papers neatly stapled together.

"I know," Langhorne said.

"You've seen the polls?"

"Candace, there are a handful of very specific channels of communication for which you serve as my protective buffer. For every other single piece of relevant information on this great big spheroid we call Earth, just go ahead and assume that I'm at least two news cycles ahead of you."

Candace's face and neck flushed at the reprimand, and she shot a quick glance at the three young men working at laptops behind her. They pretended not to notice. "I've already sowed some seeds at Reuters with an article about response bias," she said, "implying the polls are slanted against the president. We've also got that *Times* editorial comparing the Republican candidates to the cast of a reality show, and I think this would be a good time to hit with that."

As Candace outlined countermeasure strategy, Langhorne hooked his tablet computer to a projector and brought up an interactive map of the United States. "The national polls aren't the problem. They are a symptom, and they're going to get worse."

One of the young men working at his laptop spoke up, to the surprise of the other two. He wore a dress shirt and tie, but his hair was too long to be taken seriously by the Beltway crowd. "But the straw polls only show the President losing to an imaginary generic Republican," the young man said. "None of their actual candidates even comes close in a head-to-head."

"Not yet," Langhorne said. "But that's because the real candidate has yet to show himself. And when he does, the straw polls will swing wildly in his favor."

"Who?" the young man asked.

"You'll find out soon enough. But the real issue is the economy. The current administration will try to steer the conversation away, but it'll keep coming back like a bad penny." Langhorne clicked on his tablet, and the states on the projector screen changed color; some turned red, while others turned blue.

"Is this the last election?" Candace asked.

"Yes. And this," he said as he tapped the screen, changing the colors of several states, "is going to be the next election." The difference was clear: a predominance of red. "We're going to lose Nevada, Florida, North Carolina, Indiana, Minnesota, Ohio, and Pennsylvania. Don't mistake this as my opinion; barring a national tragedy, which—you might be surprised to hear—is beyond my ability to create, this is what will happen."

Candace slid off her shoes and propped her feet up on an empty chair. "If it's inevitable, then what's our plan?" she asked.

"We need to make it *less* inevitable," Langhorne said. He tapped the screen again, and a running tally of electoral votes appeared at the bottom. "Either side needs 270 electoral votes to win. If we assume that we only lose those states I mentioned, then the Republicans win, 288 to 250. That's a spread of 38. If we can swing 20 electoral votes back to us, we win, 270 to 268. Ohio would've been the perfect battleground, since no Republican has ever won the election without winning Ohio. But they've lost two electoral votes, so now they're only worth 18."

"How did they lose electoral votes?" the long-haired worker asked.

One of the other young men, buzz-cut and bespectacled, leaned in and whispered, "Census."

"That's right," Langhorne said. "Just like Congressional representatives. The population in Texas goes up, the number of electors goes up. A big chunk of New Yorkers retire and move to Florida, and their electoral votes follow. So the question is, how do we hold on to 20 votes?"

"Florida might still swing," Candace offered. "Like you said, it's an aging demographic, but a lot of the newer residents are Democrats."

"If you think you can do it, then Florida's yours," Langhorne said.

"What about Ohio and Nevada?" the long-haired worker asked. "That makes 24 votes."

"Nevada's a lost cause," Langhorne said. "But since you called it, it's yours, along with Ohio." The young man looked confused, but nodded and began typing on his laptop.

Langhorne looked at the man with the buzz-cut and glasses. Upon realizing that Langhorne was waiting for a response, the man said, "Umm... Minnesota and North Carolina together would be 25. They both have Democrats as governors, and more Democrats than Republicans in Congress."

"Good choice," Langhorne said. He turned to the last worker, a bent reed of a boy who looked lost in his own clothes. He looked like he wasn't even old enough to shave yet. "And you?" he asked.

The boy's voice was barely a whisper. "Penn-Pennsylvania," he said. "Twenty votes even."

"Okay then," Langhorne said. "Nobody picked Indiana, which is fine, because I don't think we're getting Indiana back. I want to see solid plans from each of you by next week. Candace, my office."

Langhorne headed toward what had once been the master bedroom. Candace didn't bother to put her shoes on as she followed him, his lunch in hand, and locked the door behind her.

3

Jack spent the better part of a week helping out around the house, running errands for Vera Lynn, shuttling relatives to and from the funeral parlor, and doing whatever else needed to be done. He wasn't sure if he was just doing what was expected of a son whose father had just died, or if he was wildly overcompensating to keep from looking like the neglectful jerk he felt certain everyone thought he was.

The one thing he wasn't allowed to do was make important decisions. Vera Lynn assured him that she had already worked out the details with Daddy before he died. Everything from the music at the funeral ("Lights on the Hill" by Slim Dusty) to the inscription on the headstone ("The Honorable Ray Stanley Patton; Loving Father, Respected Judge, Native Texan") was decided without any input from Jack. Vera Lynn even assumed responsibility for the eulogy. "You'll just get choked up," she told him. "Then you'll be standing there like a mute. Nobody wants to see that." Even though she was right, her words stung.

They buried him facing east on Marbletop Hill, overlooking the wide green breadth of the Texas hill country, resting for eternity between his departed wife and mother. He'd bought the plots just before Jack was born, part of his unspoken plan to keep the family together regardless of what the future held. On the other side of Jack's mother, two unmarked swaths of carefully manicured green waited, patiently, for him and Vera Lynn.

After the ceremony, she sat Jack down at the kitchen table and read the highlights from their father's will. "He left me the house," she said. "He figured you wouldn't be interested in it anyway."

"Of course," Jack said. "The house should be yours." Vera Lynn had never lived away from home before; now she would be alone in this huge, decaying shell. Jack was worried for her, but he couldn't think of a way to broach the subject without offending her.

"After all the medical bills are paid, there's not much in the way of assets. I'll send you a check for half when I get the numbers."

"That's not necessary," Jack said, waving the thought from the air.

"Yeah, it's necessary," Vera Lynn said. "It's a legal declaration. There's one other part meant for you." She lifted the paper and read aloud: "To my son John Arthur Patton, I give and bequeath all my interest in the following: the pen I used to sign my presidential elector Certificates of Vote for the 1980 election, presently located in an oak box on my bedroom dresser. It is my sincerest hope that it will serve as a reminder to him of the ideals upon which our great nation was founded, and inspiration for striving to maintain those ideals in his own life."

Vera Lynn disappeared into their father's bedroom and returned with the oak box. She slid it across the table.

"Y'know, he always thought you'd be a politician," she said.

"Really?"

"When you were barely out of diapers, he used to tell me, 'Now, you watch over your baby brother. He just might be president someday.'"

"Yeah, well... no recipe for disappointment there."

"He never held anything against you, John Arthur. Not when you wrecked his truck your senior year, not when you wasted his money changing majors at college... not even when you stopped coming for Christmas after Mom died. But you shouldn't ought to have stayed away so long."

"Goes both ways," Jack said, and snatched up the box. "I... gotta get back."

"Yeah," she said, as if she'd known the words were coming even before he did. "Don't let it hit you on the way out." She closed her eyes and rubbed her temples, preemptively shutting him out.

*   *   *

On his way back to Austin, Jack stared at the oak box poised, lid up, on his passenger seat. He couldn't shake the feeling that the pen was a message from his father, a dying wish imparted in an object rather than in the simple currency

15

of words that had often failed them. His father was asking him to *do something*.

He couldn't really expect Jack to run for president—that would be absurd. Going back to school to finish a law degree seemed equally unlikely. But Jack knew there was something, some act that would show his father—and himself—that he truly was engaged with the world. That he wasn't just some lazy fool who walked away from a promising career path so that he could sit around and doodle all day instead.

His father had done so much over the course of his life. Jack wanted to prove that he, too, could play at least some part—however tiny—in shaping the destiny of the nation. He ran a finger down the smooth black lacquer shaft of the pen, and suddenly the answer seemed so obvious.

4

THE NEXT TIME Langhorne drove out to the Harrington house, he was greeted by mounds of trash outside the back door: sagging black bags filled with finely shredded paper; stacks of empty pizza boxes; a cheap printer that had clearly been worked beyond its limit.

"Holy hell," he said once he was inside. "This place smells like a feral cat colony." The bleary-eyed staffers got the message and began to mindlessly scoop clutter from their desks.

"Everyone's been burning the midnight oil," Candace said, grabbing a can of air freshener and blasting it into the nearest heating vent. "Sorry for the trash outside. I didn't want to put it all on the curb at once since it could... raise eyebrows around here."

"There's an old dump west of town on 279," Langhorne said. "But anything that can be traced back to anyone here needs to be burned." He nodded toward the wide brick mantle on the far wall, nearly hidden behind a tangled mass of computer equipment. "That's what the fireplace is for."

As Langhorne pulled out his tablet and hooked it up to the projector, the rest of the team shifted their seats and took out clean note pads. "I'm sure that by now even Delaware has gotten word about the new Republican front-runner."

The whole team nodded. Candace said, "Governor Randell of Florida. Which means, there goes my plan to swing Florida."

Langhorne clicked on Florida on his tablet screen, and the state turned red. The other swing states—Nevada, Minnesota, Indiana, Ohio, Pennsylvania, and North Carolina—were still marked with a neutral color to signify "uncounted." The total number of electoral votes shifted, deceptively showing the Democratic incumbent with a lead of 250 to 208. "So that leaves us with six battlegrounds to secure 20 electoral votes."

Mr. Buzz-Cut—who, Langhorne had forced himself to commit to memory, was Vincent Platt—raised his hand. "What if Maine splits?"

Perhaps Platt believed the scenario was plausible, but it seemed equally likely that he just wanted to impress Langhorne by revealing his knowledge of Maine's split electoral vote system. Like Nebraska, the state offered one electoral vote to the winner of each district, with the remainder cast for the winner of the statewide popular vote. Every other state used the "winner take all" system, where the statewide popular vote getter earned all the state's electoral votes.

"If the Republican nominee was from the Northeast, that would be a concern," Langhorne said. "Maine's Second District is largely rural. But Randell's too Southern for their tastes."

The long-haired hacker, whose name Langhorne remembered as Miles something, was not to be outclassed. "So we're assuming that Nebraska's Second District is still going Democrat? They redistricted to split off Bellevue and Offutt, obviously to dilute the Democratic base."

"The president has a friend in Omaha," Langhorne said, without further elaboration.

"And are we sure Colorado is safe?" Platt asked. "The last win may have been a fluke. It usually swings red."

"Enough," Langhorne said. "I told you which battlegrounds to focus on. Six states, which give us nine possible win scenarios. Out of those nine scenarios, three involve Indiana and two involve Nevada, both of which are lost causes. That leaves us with four possibilities: win Pennsylvania, or win Ohio and North Carolina, Ohio and Minnesota, or North Carolina and Minnesota. So?" He looked at the three young staffers. "Who wants to go first?"

Platt cleared his throat. "I've got a media strategy for Minnesota that I think could swing five to eight percent of the voters."

Langhorne raised his brow and dropped his chin to his chest. "Media strategy? And what is your experience with media relations?"

Platt was caught off-guard. "Well, no direct experience, but-"

"Let me share something with you. The president has the top image-maker in D.C. developing a custom gesture repertoire for his public appearances. He's got a linguist on staff to make sure he doesn't elongate his vowels or shift his velar stops too far back in his throat when he speaks. Aside from his team of speech writers, he also has a room full of comedy writers on staff to come up with daily soundbites to feed the media machine. All of this is filtered through one person, a media savant whose real name is known by only about two dozen people in all of Washington and who carefully plans the release of every last bit of information related to the president. And *you* want to pitch media strategy." Langhorne sighed. "I think there's a fundamental misunderstanding about what we're doing here. Would anyone care to venture a guess?"

"We're here to get the president re-elected," Candace said.

"That's only half an answer," he said. "The full answer is this: we're here to get the president re-elected *using whatever means necessary.*"

Langhorne pointed to Platt. "You were Special Ops Sustainment in Afghanistan. You're an expert at planning and implementing large-scale support operations without attracting unwanted attention. And you," he continued, pointing at Miles, "hacked into Bank of America's servers last year and then freely posted the account and PIN numbers of twenty thousand customers."

Miles was taken back. "No way," he said. "That was some dude in Virginia. I read about that somewhere."

"You're right that someone else was arrested for the crime," Langhorne said. "You zombied his computer and used it as a slave to hide your tracks. Very clever, but not quite clever enough. Do you want to know why he's in jail and you're here?"

Miles flushed with humiliation and anger. The denials evaporated. "Why?"

"Because you're more valuable to us than he is." Langhorne turned to the third young man, who was still wearing clothes too big for his tiny frame. "And you are Grant Imani, also known as Grim on Carcass of Democracy—the website that broke three major political scandals in the past two years. You can, pardon the colloquialism, turn up dirt better than a pig on a truffle hunt." Grant shifted uncomfortably and tried to disappear farther into his clothes as Langhorne continued. "You all have unique talents, and we're going to need them in the coming year."

"So what is she an expert at?" Miles said, nodding toward Candace and letting the obvious insinuation hang in the air.

Candace moved to speak, but Langhorne stopped her with a single finger. "She's been personally responsible for fourteen state-level election wins and she knows more about the democratic process than most tenured political science professors." Langhorne swiftly leaned in toward Miles, never breaking his gaze as he delicately steepled the tips of his fingers on Miles's desk. "She's also been combat trained by the Mossad and can tear off a man's testicles right through his pants." Miles swallowed hard enough for everyone in the room to hear, and said nothing else.

"You may have been led to believe that this is a typical strategy think-tank. It's not. We have tools at our disposal here that most lobbyists and PACs couldn't even dream of. You have an opportunity to shape the course of American politics in a way few can. But you're never going to achieve fame or glory for your efforts. No one will ever know what you've done. If anyone does find out, a lengthy jail sentence is the most optimistic outcome you can hope for."

"So we're supposed to break the law," Platt said.

"You're supposed to free your mind from constraints about what is and what is not legal," said Langhorne. "We pay a team of lawyers lots of money to worry about those things."

The faces staring back at Langhorne were uneasy, puzzled. "Let me give you an example. In 2000, a phone bank run by Republican strategists placed calls to white Democrat-leaning households in New Jersey to convince them to vote Democrat. Why would Republicans encourage Democrats to vote Democrat? Simple: they weren't. The calls were made using exaggerated African American and Hispanic accents. They wanted to scare white voters *away* from aligning with minorities. Even if they couldn't scare the voters into going Republican, they could at least scare them away from the polls on election day. Was it illegal? Unethical? It doesn't matter, because it was effective.

"Here's another example. In 2004, there were massive voting anomalies in Ohio's presidential election... too many to list, but lots of them involved the electronic voting machines being used. The head of the company that made the machines had previously sent out a letter saying he was committed to helping the Republican president stay in office.

"One of the consultants hired to work on programming the machines was a convicted felon who spent four years in prison for running a computer-based embezzlement scam. Three other executives were later sued by the SEC for committing fraud during this same time period. The company paid twenty-five million dollars in a settlement. In 2008, a web designer and Republican strategist who worked on the 2004 and 2006 elections—and was reportedly eager to spill his guts to a reporter about voter fraud in Ohio—was killed in a plane crash. He was the only passenger.

"Investigations of those suspicious occurrences—and literally hundreds of others that have been documented—did absolutely nothing to change the outcome of the Ohio vote, which went Republican by a slim margin and ultimately decided the presidency. In elections, more than anything else in the world, this is true: it is better to ask forgiveness than permission."

Langhorne turned his attention back to the election map. "Now then. Six battleground states, with only four worth pursuing. Ideas?"

Grant tentatively poked his hand into the air. "Pennsylvania's had lots of problems with its voting machines. Most of them are five years old now, which is standard lifespan. They'll probably be replacing them next year. If we could control the source of the new machines..."

"We could use a shelf corporation to set up our own voting machine vendor," Candace offered.

Langhorne shook his head. "Those sorts of contracts are strictly friends and family plan."

"Huh?"

"If you're not a friend or relative of the governor, you'll never even get a chance to bid on the job."

The room fell silent. Desperate eyes darted back and forth. Finally, Miles began to mumble something.

"Speak up," said Langhorne.

"There's this tech I've been playing with... it can transmit code through an optical scanner."

"How does it work?"

"It exploits a weakness in the character recognition software."

"And how is this useful to us?" Candace asked.

"I've noticed that a lot of districts are moving to optical scan voting machines..."

A half-smile crept across Langhorne's face.

Candace tried to follow along. "So what does that mean?"

"It means someone could infect voting machines with a virus," Langhorne said. "And they could do this by scanning a dummy ballot, which loads the code onto the machine."

"And that breaks the machine, or what?" Candace asked.

"The right kind of virus could alter the vote count within the machine without anyone ever knowing," said Langhorne.

"Yeah," Miles said. "Well, in theory. I'd still have to figure out some stuff."

"Make it happen," Langhorne said. "I want to see a prototype by next week. Anyone else?" The others remained silent. "I expect ideas from everyone. Think about your strengths and work from there. I know you have it in you—that's why you were picked for this team." Langhorne unhooked his tablet and strode to his office without another word. Candace trailed behind like a petal caught upon a breeze.

"I think it's working," Candace said after she closed the door behind her.

"What's that?" Langhorne asked.

"This whole disapproving father relationship you have with them. They really want to please you."

"They could please me by delivering some goddamn results." He settled in behind his desk. "Maybe this isn't the team."

"It is," she insisted. "They just needed some motivation."

"They've got one week to give me something I can work with. Otherwise I'm pulling the plug."

She slipped behind his chair and laid a hand on his shoulder. "Don't worry, they'll come through." She began massaging his neck, and he melted into his chair.

"You could've told me it was going to be Randell," Candace said. "I wouldn't have wasted my time on a Florida strategy."

"I wanted them to have to do the heavy lifting," he said.

"And thanks for the Mossad line, by the way."

"From now on I'm betting Miles will cross his legs every time you walk by."

She giggled and dropped her face to his, exhaling warmly into his ear. She brushed it with her lips, then tugged the lobe with her teeth. He reached up and placed his hand under her jaw, more forceful than affectionate. He held her face and turned to look her dead in the eye. "One week," he said.

She nodded, so slightly that it could have been mistaken for a shudder of fear.

5

Jack had expected the Travis County Republican Party headquarters to be some stately stone edifice that stood, cold and imposing, in the shadow of the Capitol Building on Congress Avenue, right in the pulsing heart of Austin. Instead, following the commands of his GPS, he found himself pulling into a nondescript industrial park on the eastern outskirts of town. The headquarters were located in a dull squat brick of a building that housed, among other things, a pest control service, a masonry company, two real estate agencies, and a bail bondsman.

The County Chair was Emmet Washburn, a stout man whose neck looked permanently razor-burned. His plump, soft hand disguised a vise-like grip that told Jack in no uncertain terms, *I could bring you to your knees if I wanted to.*

"How can I help you, son?" Emmet asked.

"I'm trying to find out what I need to do to become an

elector," Jack said.

"You mean delegate."

"No, I mean elector. As in, member of the electoral college."

Emmet let out a wheezy laugh. "Why not just run for Congress? Your odds are about the same, and you'd at least get a paycheck out of it."

"My father was County Chair in Nobles for about twenty years. I'm trying to honor his dying wish."

Emmet narrowed his eyes. "Nobles. You're Ray Patton's boy?"

"Yes sir."

"Well, how about that. Ray was a hell of a man. I'm sorry to hear he passed on." Emmet drummed his fingers on his desk for a moment, seemingly sizing up Jack. "Tell me about this dying wish, then," he said.

Jack told it all, even more than he had planned. He told Emmet about his childhood trip to Washington and how much it had meant, and about his father's pride at casting his electoral vote for Reagan. He told Emmet about how his relationship with his father had deteriorated, and that he had never really gotten the chance to make things right.

"You got quite a story," Emmet said. "But there's a way things work in the party. You put in your time, and eventually you get your turn. Being chosen as an elector is one of the highest honors you can achieve. We got people been Precinct Chairs for thirty-five years and they ain't had a chance to be electors. Now maybe we can get you started as a Precinct Chair—we've got some vacancies—and when the time comes, you'll get your chance."

This was not at all what Jack had hoped to hear. He wanted

to fulfill his father's wish as soon as possible—not sometime in the future when party leaders finally decided that his turn had come up. "There's no quicker way?" he asked.

"Son, don't take this the wrong way... your daddy was something special, but out here in Travis County, nobody knows you from the milkman. You might have better luck if you were back in Nobles."

"What do you mean, back in Nobles?"

"Every Congressional district chooses their own nominees for elector, and then there are some chosen by the state party heads. With your daddy's reputation, you might could sway some folks at the caucus come primary time."

"But I've lived in Austin for the past ten years," Jack said. "I imagine there's some sort of residency issue, right?"

"Maybe not. What district you live in?"

Jack stared blankly. "Uh... I should probably know that."

Emmet smirked. "Point out on the map here where you live," he said, tapping his desk. Underneath the glass surface was a multi-colored map of Travis County and the surrounding area. The colored regions paid little regard to city limits; broad pastel swaths became jagged intermingled swirls where they met in the city center.

Jack found his neighborhood and pointed it out. "All right then," Emmet said, and clapped his beefy hands together. "See, even though you live in Austin, you're still part of the Twenty-First District, which goes all the way out to Nobles and then some."

"That's good then, I guess," Jack said. "But why is Austin split up like that? Shouldn't all of Austin be its own district?"

"Well, now you get into a population issue," he said. "Austin is so big that it would have to be more than one district. So then it's just a matter of making sure that the districts are an accurate reflection of the state as a whole, which is predominantly Republican. We try to balance urban and rural areas so that there isn't one group whose interests dominate. Of course, the Democrats would just love to slice and dice the map so that the minorities control more districts, which gives them more seats in Congress. But the Democrats don't control the state legislature, and like some Yankee once said, to the victor go the spoils."

Jack tried to convince himself that it all made some kind of sense. "I never realized this was all such a complicated business," he said.

"Just wait till primary season comes along," Emmet said. He glanced past Jack's shoulder toward the office lobby, and his face brightened for a brief moment. He abruptly leaned forward and held out his hand for Jack to shake once again. "Good luck to ya, son," he said. The message was friendly but clear: *We're done here.*

"Thank you for the advice," Jack said, enduring the crushing grip one last time. But even more painful was the thought of heading back to Nobles, hat in hand, to ask the town he had forsaken to help him fulfill a promise that might well be—as he had just discovered—nothing more than a pipe dream.

*   *   *

"Well hell, the prodigal bum returns." Jack's best friend and employee of undetermined role, Silas Wernicke, sat with his feet propped up on his desk, keyboard balanced on his belly, bouncing a tennis ball off the wall. "We sent a search party off to Nobles looking for you, but they died of boredom."

"Yeah, you look like you're keeping plenty busy," Jack said. He turned to Marlene, who was trimming out shapes of colored paper. "Has he got you doing his work?" he asked.

"I'm making Christmas cards," she said without looking up. "God, elves suck."

Jack set his computer bag in an empty chair and looked around the office. Nothing had changed since he left nearly two weeks before. "So no new projects?"

"Be glad for that," Silas said. "I can keep your seat warm while you're gone, but sooner or later, clients are gonna realize that I ain't you."

"You can handle clients just fine."

"Sure, I can trace over somebody's old logo in Illustrator, clean it up a bit. But the second somebody comes walking through that door looking to develop a new brand identity, I'm probably gonna start talking gibberish and then throw up. Just so you know."

"How'd Polar Air come off?"

"Fine," Silas said. "You pretty much had that finished before you left. Marlene already invoiced 'em. Didn't you Marlene?"

"Shut up... I'm cutting elves."

"There you go," Silas said. "Well-oiled machine, we are. The precision instrument that is Roundabout Design. Did you know that I actually have quartz movement? I get it from my mom."

Jack just rolled his eyes. "Guess I'd better try and scare up some business so we can pay rent next month," Jack said, and headed toward his modest office.

As he moved to close the door, Marlene at last looked up from her cuttings. "Welcome back," she said.

On his desk, Jack found a single message scrawled in Marlene's hand: "Call whats-her-face." After the divorce, when Jack was at his lowest point, Silas and Marlene vowed to ban his ex-wife's name from ever being mentioned at the office. It was a gesture of solidarity that had gone on so long, it was unlikely to ever be reversed.

Jack picked up the phone and his fingers punched the keys by muscle memory before he could even picture the numbers in his head. She had kept the same cell phone number after their divorce, and for some reason it irked him. That string of numbers was part of their life together, and in his mind, it should have gone down with the ship.

"Jack?" said the voice on the other end.

"Hi Anna."

"I just heard about Ray. I'm so sorry."

"It was a long time coming. You know."

A snowy pause. "Why didn't you call and tell me?"

"I... didn't know I was supposed to," he said.

"Jesus, Jack, he was my father-in-law for ten years."

"Nine and a half."

"Whatever. I just... I would've liked a chance to say good-bye."

"I just figured you've moved on," he said. It came out sounding meaner than he had intended.

"That's not fair," she said, and he could hear her voice quiver. "How many nights did I spend talking to him on the phone when you pretended not to be home? I talked to him more those last five years than you did. I deserved to know."

"I'm sorry," he said.

"And Vera Lynn hates my guts, so there's no way she would call and let me know. I was counting on you."

"I said I'm sorry."

"Yeah. Me too." Before she hung up, he heard the words echo faintly one more time. "Me too."

6

THE FOLLOWING WEEK was unseasonably cold in the Northeast, and as Langhorne made the drive out to the Harrington house, the dirty slush of the city gave way to a thin, even dusting of snow that settled like grace on the trees and buildings that lined the highway. He passed by two minor car accidents along the way, probably caused by locals who had forgotten—in less than a year—the dangers of winter driving. Langhorne saw similarly shallow memories in Washington all the time; it was downright epidemic.

The house was filled with nervous energy when he arrived. Platt was flipping through presentation slides on his tablet as Candace aimed the projector at the wall and adjusted it. Miles's desk was buried beneath the guts of a disassembled vote scanner; he was furiously typing code, hoping that Langhorne wouldn't notice him yet. Grant sat at his tidy desk, oddly serene, like a death-row inmate who had lost his last appeal and resigned himself to his fate.

"This is it, people," Langhorne said. "In order to keep this team funded, we need a plan today. So..." Langhorne dropped into an executive chair and waved his arm with a flourish. "Spare me no riches."

Platt went first. He clicked on his tablet and the projector flashed the words "Disruption Effect" onto the blank wall. As he spoke, he flipped quickly through several slides that featured colorful graphs and charts that supported his points. "According to a PoliStrat poll," Platt said, "thirty-two percent of Pennsylvanians don't know their polling location before election week. That means they rely heavily on the Internet and local party offices on election day to find out where to vote. A disruption effect could be enough to keep Republican votes away."

"What do you suggest?" Langhorne asked.

"We jam the phone banks at the local GOP office and launch a DoS attack on the state party web page starting two days before the election. We can do it with a staff of probably twenty or thirty. Each user enslaves a certain number of vulnerable computers and directs them all to access the target web page at the same time, flooding their servers." Platt switched slides to show a graphic illustrating a denial of service attack; it depicted a single computer splitting into ten virtual computers, all of them sending out arrows aimed at a single box labeled "Republican Party of Pennsylvania Web Servers."

"I'm estimating we get between one-half and one percent dropoff from voters who give up on trying to find out where they're supposed to vote. That doesn't sound like much, but with over three million registered Republicans and millions of undecideds, we're talking about tens of thousands of votes. Could be enough to sway it."

Everyone looked to Langhorne expectantly. "Two problems," Langhorne said. "There are still plenty of bipartisan resources to let people know where to vote. Also, and I'm sure you know this, the disruption effect is far more likely to dissuade potential Democrat votes than Republican votes. Which means you can bet the other side is already planning on doing this to us, and doing it better. There's nothing new here... nothing to help us gain the advantage."

Platt nodded his understanding, but looked inwardly devastated.

"Speaking of something new," Langhorne continued, "Miles? How's the vote-scanner virus coming along?"

Miles nervously shuffled some loose electronic components on his desk. "I, uh, I'm still fine-tuning the code, but I'm definitely getting results."

"What kind of results?"

"I can corrupt the scanner's character recognition software, which makes it unusable. But rewriting the code to make it do what we want is... trickier."

"That tricky part is the only thing that makes the plan worth doing," Langhorne said. "How far away are you?"

"I... don't know."

"That's a problem," said Langhorne.

"Hey, it's not like I can crowdsource this, okay? It's just me, sitting here in a room, staring at Grant for eighteen hours a day."

"This could still be useful, though, right?" Candace offered. "What if we used this to crash scanners in Republican strongholds, to force longer lines and hand-counting? Make the lines long enough, and some people are bound to leave."

Langhorne shook his head. "If we wanted to, we could fry a voting machine's motherboard from a hundred yards away and no one would have any idea what happened. But crashing scanners doesn't get us anything. A hand-count in a Republican precinct is still going to favor the Republican candidate.

"The only meaningful part of the plan is changing the scanner's vote-tabulation software without anyone knowing until later. We already have people who can hack a touch-screen vote machine so that the votes can be redistributed any way we want. The only problem is that our people need about five minutes alone with each machine to make it happen. The only feasible way to do it is before election day, but the Republican Party is funding round-the-clock security on machines headed for battle precincts. They're doing it through the machine manufacturers, so it looks impartial. Which means that only *they* have access to the machines from factory to polling place. And they know how to hack as well as we do. Finding a way to reprogram the machines on election day is just about our only chance to use them to swing things back in our favor."

"I'm not saying I can't do it," Miles said. "I just can't do it, like, right now."

"That's a shame because, like, right now is precisely when I need to see some results to keep this team funded." Langhorne swiveled his chair toward Grant. "Should I even bother to ask, or are we going zero for three today?"

Grant cleared his throat meekly. "At first, I tried to think of ways we could turn their own base against them. Maybe faked audio clips of the Governor Randell soliciting a gay prostitute, leaked emails where he supports socialized medicine, that kind of thing. Then I remembered something Miles said the other day." He turned to Miles, who looked surprised to find out that he played a part in Grant's proposal. "I asked you what the most vulnerable part of any security system was, and you said-"

"People," Miles finished. "People are always the weakest link."

"Right. And we've been trying to think of all these high-tech ways of tilting the tables back in our favor. But what if it was actually much easier than that?" Grant slid a thin stapled packet across the desk to Langhorne. The cover sheet read, in tiny, unassuming print, "Project Faithless."

*　　　　　　*　　　　　　*

When the meeting was over, Langhorne drove back across the bridge to Annapolis, but instead of heading west to Washington, he went north, skirting Baltimore and continuing on into Pennsylvania. It was after dark by the time he reached Gettysburg. Along East Cemetery Hill, where stone monuments presided over the ghosts of thousands of Confederate and Union dead, a small group of tourists with candle lanterns stood in the bitter cold, listening to a woman in period dress tell tales of the paranormal.

The Gettysburg house was a two-story faux colonial built in the 1960s, part of a quiet suburb west of downtown. The houses sat on generous lots, just far enough apart for an owner to enjoy complete privacy from his or her neighbors.

Langhorne slipped his sedan into the garage and was met by a tall, balding man in a sweater and moccasins. He had eyes like an owl, a trait made all the more noticeable by his frequent blinking. "We weren't expecting you till tomorrow," the man said.

"Let's talk," Langhorne replied.

They headed into the house, past several professionally-dressed workers typing away diligently in well-kept rows of desks. Most did not acknowledge him as he passed, but a young brunette smiled at Langhorne and whispered, "Hello, Mister Bierce."

The two men entered a richly appointed study with built-in mahogany bookcases. Instead of ancient, gilt-edged volumes of literature, the shelves were lined with stacks of papers and overstuffed manila folders. "We're seeing good things with Brendon's targeted web campaigns," the man said. "I think it's really going to bring some disillusioned supporters back to the fold." He opened a pizza box on his desk and turned it toward Langhorne. "Slice? You gotta be hungry after that drive."

"Mike... I'm shutting you down."

Mike closed the pizza box and sank back into his chair. "So I guess the Harrington team must've struck gold then, huh?"

Langhorne said nothing.

"Yeah, I know about Harrington. I also know about Fredericksburg, and what happened to them. How many other teams are out there, Ron?"

"The name is Bierce," Langhorne said through tight lips.

"God damn it, Ron, I've known you for fifteen years. I'm not going to call you by some code name. So how's it supposed to go down? Electrical fire in the middle of the night? Home invasion gone bad?"

Langhorne cocked his head toward the closed door for a moment, then spoke just above a whisper. "Your team will board a small turbo-prop charter at Gettysburg Regional Airport at five-twenty tomorrow morning. The plane will be headed for Harrisburg International. Tell your team that they're getting a well-deserved break for the holidays, and that the operation will resume the first week of January."

"Except it won't," Mike said. "They're not gonna make it to Harrisburg, are they?"

Langhorne said nothing.

"I can't let you do it," Mike said. "These are good people. They've done nothing but dedicate themselves to the job you gave them."

"Is it the brunette?" Langhorne asked.

"What?"

"You've obviously grown close to your team, Mike. But there's one in particular, isn't there? That's why you've lost your nerve."

"Maybe I just realized that I don't want to be involved in your sleazy dealings anymore. I don't care how much you pay me."

"Politics is a dirty business, friend," Langhorne said. "So you're out then?"

Mike nodded.

"You sure about that? Once you've made that call, I can't protect you."

Mike squinted his eyes. "That sounds like a threat. Just know that if anybody comes after me, I'll spill your shit across the front page of every major paper in the country."

"Well then." Langhorne stood and headed for the door. "I guess there's nothing else to be said."

"What'd they come up with?" Mike asked. "The Harrington team. It must be something pretty damn great, right?"

"We'll find out next November," Langhorne said as he disappeared down the hall.

*   *   *

Two days later, *The Patriot-News* ran two brief articles on separate pages in its Local & State section. The first detailed a small-plane crash that happened in the thickly-wooded state game lands southwest of Harrisburg. According to the article, it was a small turbo-prop charter out of Gettysburg that reported engine trouble less than a minute before it went down. The pilot and all five passengers, described as consultants for an environmental lobbying group, were killed upon impact.

The second article reported a deadly single-car accident that occurred in the wee hours along northbound U.S. Route 15 between Harrisburg and Gettysburg. According to local police, the accident was attributed to icy conditions and driver error. The article was accompanied by two thumbnail-sized pictures of the victims, both killed upon impact: a balding, former political science professor from Syracuse University named Michael Cupertino; and his passenger, a lovely young brunette from Utica named Kaylee Kincaid.

7

Jack tried to keep focused on work, but invariably found himself studying precinct maps and poring over Republican Party rules booklets, trying to make sense of it all. He called his sister and told her his plan. When he was done, he sat in silence for what felt like a minute waiting for her to respond. He thought he heard sobbing, but it could have just as easily been static from the old house's decaying phone lines. Finally, Vera Lynn said, "I think that would be all right, Jack."

A few days later, Vera Lynn called him at his office. "We've got a Club meeting this Saturday," she said. "You should stop by and get to know some folks." The "Club" was the Republican Club, and Jack knew it was the core of party activity in Nobles. As a child he had spent many evenings perched upon his father's knee down at the old headquarters building, as Club members shared potluck and informally set the course for the party without any need at all for motions or votes.

Having already been shot down at the proverbial velvet-roped entrance, the Club was precisely the secret side-door into the party that Jack knew he needed.

The Republican Club meeting was at the Nobles Community Center, a long stone building just off the town square that looked too modern and well-kept to fit in with the rest. Once inside, Jack realized that the building was monstrous. "I bet you could fit half the town in here," he said to Vera Lynn. "Has this thing ever been filled, even once?"

She shrugged. "Came close with the railroad festival, I think. But most of the time it just sits empty."

About fifty people milled around the far end of the meeting hall, next to a long banquet table covered in mismatched plates, trays, and crock pots. As they approached, Jack wondered where on earth he could possibly set down the huge platter of sandwiches that he carried for his sister. A tall, egg-shaped woman in a salmon pantsuit waved toward them. Vera Lynn whispered, "That's Dottie Jenkins, the party chair. You remember her?"

Jack did remember her. He went to school with her youngest brother, Gail. As Jack recalled, the poor kid spent most of junior high being picked on about his name, which Jack assumed was probably intended to honor some long-dead uncle or grandfather. But whenever big sister Dottie was around, the heckling fell to a hush. She had sprouted early, and as far as Jack could tell now, kept on sprouting.

"Why hello, Jack," Dottie said. "It's been some years."

"Sure has," he said. "Good to see you again, Dottie. How are your brothers?" As soon as the words came out he saw Vera Lynn's features pinch up, and realized he shouldn't have asked.

Dottie exhaled like a balloon deflating. "One's in and out of jail, and the other's in and out of a job. Can't tell those boys anything," she said.

Jack nodded sympathetically, and after an awkward moment, said, "Where should I put the sandwiches?"

"Anywhere's fine, hon," Dottie said, and commenced chatting with Vera Lynn. But as Jack had already seen, there was simply no room on the buffet table for the platter. He glanced around, hoping someone would sense his desperation and offer to help. Instead he got a few terse head nods and nothing more. That was how it would be, he realized. He was now the outsider, regardless of how many years he had lived there.

He spotted a few nearly empty plates and used his free hand to consolidate several random snacks onto a single dish. Then he removed the empties and shifted every other plate, one at a time, like a slide tile puzzle until he had cleared a single large spot. At last he was able to set the platter down and massage his aching wrist. He couldn't help thinking that politics might be hard, but potlucks were downright brutal.

He looked up to find the chattering crowd drifting toward him, with his sister at the crest. Vera Lynn spoke up above the chatter, and everyone else fell silent. "For anybody who doesn't already know," she said, "this here's my little brother Jack. He hasn't been around much lately, but he's hoping to honor our daddy by mending some fences."

She fell silent, and for a moment Jack thought she was done. "Some of y'all might remember back in Eighty-Three," she continued, "when that tornado touched down on the edge of town, tore the roof off the Texaco." A majority of heads bobbed in assent, and murmurs of remembrance briefly filled the room before Vera Lynn continued.

"Me and Jack was in the living room watching *The People's Court* when we heard the siren go off. That was back when you only heard about a tornado on the TV after it was long gone. Daddy came barrelin' out of his study and barked at us to follow him out to the storm cellar. The rain and hail was already so bad that we couldn't hardly see across the street. Well, by the time I got to the cellar door and turned around, Jack was gone. Just plain disappeared.

"Now, Jack wasn't always one to do what he was told. In fact, you could just about always count on him to do the opposite of what he was told. Just ask Nancy." Vera Lynn gestured to an elderly woman in the back of the room. "She spent Jack's whole tenth grade year trying to get him to stop capitalizing adjectives in English class. Nancy, I'm sorry to say that he still does it, and I'm pretty sure it's just to spite you." Nancy wagged a gnarled finger at Jack, and the hall filled with laughter.

"Anyhow," Vera Lynn continued, "when Daddy realized that Jack wasn't in the cellar, he let out a stream of curses that would've made Lyndon Johnson blush. He threw open the door and ran out screaming, 'God damn it, Jack! Get your ass back here!' We could feel the tornado gettin' closer... it was like a freight train, so powerful it could damn near shake the teeth loose from your head.

"Just when I thought we couldn't wait any longer for him, I saw Jack comin' back across the street. But he wasn't alone: he was practically dragging old Mrs. Wiegert with him, putting his shirt over her head to keep the hail off. She was a widow that lived across the road from us. She didn't get around too well, and she was just about a hair shy of being stone deaf.

"See, Jack knew she didn't have a cellar. He also knew she couldn't hear the siren. Without giving it a second thought, he ran off into the storm to find Mrs. Wiegert and bring her back to somewhere safe. Even if y'all never knew anything else about my brother... well, I'd hope that's enough."

As if to break the spell she had cast over the crowd, Vera Lynn clapped her hands together once, sharply. It reverberated through the cavernous hall. "Now, it looks like we still got lots of deviled eggs and potato salad to get through, so let's not make Helen carry all that food back home, okay? Dig in!"

After that, the group warmed up noticeably to Jack, and conversation began to flow. A few seemed interested in hearing about his graphic design business, while others gently prodded for information about his relationship status. Much to his surprise, not a single person at the Republican Club meeting talked politics, which made it difficult for Jack to gauge the potential for carrying out his plan to become an elector. He kept thinking about what Emmet had said: *You put in your time, and eventually you get your turn.*

When he finally had a brief moment alone with Vera Lynn, he said, "That was some story."

"Just said what came to mind," she said.

"Well, you managed to turn me from black sheep to native son in about two minutes flat. But you know-"

Before he could finish, an elderly woman with a hairdo as stiff and delicate as cotton candy came up and placed a cool, withered hand on Jack's cheek. She smiled wistfully and said, "My, but don't you have your daddy's face."

8

Langhorne flew into Austin two days in advance of the rest of his team. He made a habit of keeping his travel agenda to himself, and he only flew large commercial passenger planes. After all, accidents on charter craft were far too common.

From the airport, he drove west into the city and headed north on Interstate 35, across Town Lake and up toward the State Capitol. He had been looking for a house not far from the Capitol, but its close proximity to the University of Texas meant that, between students and state lobbyists, there were few suitable properties available.

He eventually found a house about half a mile east of the Capitol, on the other side of I-35, which was in many ways a different world from the rest of downtown. It was an older two-story house, a sturdy American Foursquare that backed up to a cemetery. There were a few sorority houses and student rentals in the area, so any late-night activity or high number of occupants would probably go unnoticed. Not to mention the fact that Texas would be the last place anyone would look for Langhorne and his team anyway.

As Langhorne approached the small covered porch, the front door opened. A young man in a gray shirt with a burnt-orange tie waved to Langhorne. "Mister Harte?"

"What are you doing here?" Langhorne asked.

"I'm Scott Durban, your Realtor," the young man said, holding out his hand.

Langhorne took it reluctantly. "I know who you are," he said. "Escrow closed last week."

"Yeah, I was just doing a final check on those upgrades you asked for. We had the window guys install polycarbonate storm panels on all the windows. Those things are so strong they could stop a bullet."

"Really," Langhorne said.

"Totally removable, but we left them on so you could check 'em out. Storm season doesn't really start for a few months yet, so you can take 'em down if you want."

"They're fine," he said.

"Also, that team came by to reinforce the down-stairs bed-room closet like you wanted. Cinder-block interior walls, so you lost a little square footage on that, vault door that locks from the inside, separate underground power and phone lines... that's what took the longest, I imagine. Guys just finished everything this morning, so I figured I should check it all over before you got here."

"How did you know when I would get here?" Langhorne asked.

Scott shrugged and flashed a too-bright smile. "I didn't.

Guess I've just got great timing."

Langhorne stepped inside the front door and began to close it. "Thank you. I'm sure everything is fine."

Scott stopped the door with his foot. "Wait. Mister Harte, I just wanted to say that... I know you're not from around here, and I know people hear lots of scary stories about the weather, but tornadoes are pretty uncommon in the city. You seem worried, considering all the precautions you're taking, so I just wanted to put your mind at ease."

"I appreciate that," Langhorne said. "I feel safer already. And since you're here, I'll go ahead and take your copy of the key."

After Scott left, Langhorne performed a thorough security sweep of the house. When it came up clean, he spent the rest of the afternoon installing his own bugs and cameras in every room except the downstairs bedroom, which would serve as both his office and living space.

The team members trickled in, jet-lagged and excessively clothed for the mild weather, over the next two days. Candace was first, and Langhorne briefed her on the security measures he'd set up for their new headquarters. He gave Candace the task of determining the layout of the workspace and living quarters. The rest of the original team followed several hours later.

"You'll be working in the downstairs living room," she told them. "Miles and Grant, you're sharing the first bedroom on the right after you go up the stairs."

"Sharing?" Miles asked, and pointed to Grant. "This dude's got a deviated septum. How am I supposed to sleep next to that?"

"Earplugs," Candace said. "Vincent, you'll be in the second bedroom on the right."

Miles let out a protesting huff. "He gets his own room? Why's that?"

"He doesn't get his own room," Candace said.

Grant put the pieces together. "The team is expanding."

"Two new members," Candace said. "Just to round out the skill set."

When they arrived, the other team members got almost no information about them beyond their names: Fleming Chambers and Vig Lindholm. Fleming was an ethereally pretty brunette who seemed impossible to pin an age to; Vig had the height, build, and commanding presence of an athlete, matched with the hair of a 1970s Scandinavian film star. He wore a black waist pack that made him look like a tourist.

"So what do you guys do?" Miles asked.

"Field work," said Fleming, and left it at that.

After everyone had settled in, Langhorne wasted no time in setting their course. "I know you've all read the original plan written by Grant," he said. "And I imagine you all have the same question burning in your minds: why in the hell are we in Texas?"

Miles and Vincent nodded. The new team members sat still as stone.

"Grant's plan was good, but Pennsylvania was the wrong state for it. First, the candidates themselves choose their presidential electors in Pennsylvania, so we're dealing with a much smaller pool of targets. Second, we need a state with a large pool of electors to give us room to be selective. Third, the only way this plan can work is if we completely blindside the other guys, hit them where they least expect it. If they get even a whiff of what we're doing, it's over.

"We're in Texas because no one expects us to be. The majority of all campaign money and resources will be focused in six battleground states. Fighting tooth and claw for that razor-thin margin that tilts the field one way or the other. All eyes will be watching those districts, those polling places.

"Texas hasn't been a battleground state for years. It went Republican by twelve points in the last presidential election, and that's despite a substantial minority population. Texas has two hundred fifty-four counties, more than any other state... and only twenty-eight of those counties vote Democrat. The president isn't going to waste his time campaigning here, and only a fool would entertain a plan that involves a Democrat taking Texas anytime within the next twenty years.

"Which makes me the king of fools," Langhorne said. "Especially since so many people are assuming that the president will be re-elected. They think that despite how bad things are, enough Americans will realize that things could be far worse if the other side gets their way. They think we don't need a secret weapon to win.

"They are wrong. And when the time comes, every one of you will be personally responsible for preserving the presidency."

Miles starting clapping tentatively, but stopped when no one else joined in.

"Now some house rules," Langhorne said. "This is not 'Project Faithless.' It's not 'Project' anything. Names are pointless and only serve to create a record that can be used against us later. No one outside this room will know the full extent of what we're doing, and no one inside this room will be working on anything else. This is not a project... for the better part of the next year, this is your life.

"If you're called upon to do field work, never, ever refer to this house by location or address. Simply call it the Nexus. You must carry one of these with you at all times." Langhorne held up a small clip-on device. "It's a GPS tracker that records your location every three seconds and transmits it back to here. It's for your safety in the case of... unforeseen circumstances."

"Where's yours?" Miles asked Langhorne.

"That would be unnecessary," he said.

"But what if something happens and you go missing?"

"If I go missing," Langhorne said, "this whole operation vanishes."

"Trackers are fine and all," said Platt, "but if you want us to be safe, how about you give us guns?"

"You'll receive guns if necessary," Langhorne said. "But they will not be loaded."

"Doesn't that kind of limit their usefulness?"

"There's only one reason to use a gun: to get someone to do something. That person won't know the gun is empty, so it doesn't matter."

"What if we find ourselves in danger?" asked Platt.

"You improvise," Langhorne said. "Here's the problem with guns: as soon as you put a bullet in somebody, it becomes clear to the rest of the world exactly how that person died. This leads to the inevitable question: Why? And the last thing we want is people asking why.

"That leads to another important point. When you're out

in the field dealing with electors, it is critical that you make each person believe they are the only one being approached. It will be much easier to get the votes we need if the people involved don't know the real stakes."

Langhorne handed out small manila envelopes to Miles, Platt, and Grant. "Here are your new identities." Each contained a Texas driver's license, a Social Security card, credit cards, and assorted other common items like grocery store loyalty cards and gym memberships.

"Hold on," Miles said. "My new secret identity has the same first name as me."

"Yes," said Langhorne. "You three are new to undercover work, and it's better to stick as close to the truth as possible. It cuts down on the number of lies you have to keep track of."

"Why don't they get secret identities?" Platt asked, nodding toward Fleming and Vig.

"They're already using theirs," Candace said.

"Sweet, I'm a video game programmer," Miles said. He turned to Candace. "What's your secret identity?"

"I'm a lobbyist for the U.S. Chamber of Commerce."

"What happens if someone calls there to check up on you?"

"They'll find out that I'm a lobbyist for the U.S. Chamber of Commerce."

"Really."

"Really," she said.

"How did... never mind. I don't understand most of what's going on here, do I?"

Candace shook her head solemnly, as if breaking the news about the Tooth Fairy to a child.

"If you need to enter a public building or place of business,"

Langhorne continued, "be aware of security cameras. Always wear a hat, and hide as many distinguishing traits as possible. Miles, that would include your hair.

"If you need money, just ask Candace. If you need a lot of money, we'll need to route it from a shell corporation to an account in Anguilla and have it brought by courier, so we need at least three business days' notice."

Langhorne consulted a notepad, making sure he covered everything. "Your computer terminals do not have local storage. All files are saved to an encrypted server in an undisclosed location. Loading and saving may take slightly longer than you're used to, so keep file sizes as small as possible."

Langhorne looked up from his notepad. "Any questions?" He waited only a brief moment before adding, "Good. Candace, my office."

Candace followed him inside and closed the door.

"Where are we with research?" he asked.

"The oppo team is wondering, of course, why they're in Texas digging up dirt on state legislators instead of being in Florida trying to nail Randell to the wall."

"Tell them they don't get paid to wonder. What have they turned up?"

She pulled out a dozen manila folders and flipped through them. "Plenty, but I think there's one clear front-runner." She held out a folder with the name "Donnie Lee Haycombe" written on the tab.

Langhorne flipped through the pages in silence, then handed it back to Candace. "This is our guy," he said.

9

Jack's success at the Republican Club meeting led to an invite to a chili cook-off two weeks later. It felt to Jack like things were moving slowly... too slowly. But Vera Lynn assured him that he would be part of every party function in town, able to plant his name in everyone's head for the eventual selection of delegates. "Remember," she told him, "this ain't Austin. Folks here don't operate on city speed. You gotta be patient."

The chili cook-off was held at the fairgrounds outside of town, a desolate expanse of mesquite and granite between the cowboy church and the county jail. The weather, depending upon who you asked, was "uncooperative," "like being showered with freezing spit," or "downright perfect for some pipin' hot chili."

Vera Lynn had convinced the Club to choose Jack as one of the secret judges for the cook-off, since his lack of familiarity with the participants would afford him a certain level of objectivity. That was the reasoning, anyway; Vera Lynn still had very explicit instructions for how he should vote.

"Don't pick Rutherford to win," she said in a low voice as they surveyed Cooks' Alley, a hastily arranged row of tents covering tables with portable stoves and crock pots. Jack recognized Rutherford Brock tending to one of the crock pots. Rutherford had been one of his father's good friends. He wore a blousy Hawaiian print shirt, and it seemed to Jack that he had lost quite a bit of weight.

"Why not?" Jack asked.

"He's on some kind of health kick since his bypass, so he's making turkey chili."

"What's wrong with that?"

"This is a red chili cook-off, not some foo-foo Austin soiree. Last thing you need is to come in looking like a city boy who likes his cooking all fancy."

"Fine then. No on Rutherford."

"And don't pick Bill Hibbert either. He's been goin' on and on about this beef he imported from Japan. Can you believe that? If he won, he'd be impossible to be around."

"Got it."

"And you can't let Shelley Hawkins finish in the top three. That's a long story goes back about five years, you don't want to hear the details, but trust me."

"How about you just tell me who I should vote for?" Jack said.

Vera Lynn looked surprised. "Just pick the one that tastes the best," she said.

Before judging began, Dottie Jenkins introduced the local candidates for the upcoming election. Most, like the Tax Assessor and the various Constables, were incumbents running unopposed; events like these were just a way to cement community relations. Jack dutifully pressed palms and made small talk with all the candidates, including a slightly imbalanced elderly man who insisted he was running for Commissioner, though no one else seemed to take him seriously.

The county sheriff, Hil Sempel, was a red-haired barrel on stilts. His bulbous nose looked like it had been chewed on by a raccoon. "Sorry to hear about your daddy," Sheriff Sempel said to Jack as they shook hands. Jack normally thought of the word "daddy" as something a girl might say—Vera Lynn was the only other person he knew who used it—but somehow Sempel owned it. "He meant a lot to a lot of people in this town," he continued. Jack sensed in Sempel's demeanor a few unsaid words at the end of that sentence: "...*but not me.*"

Next to the sheriff stood a younger man, wearing nothing but a t-shirt and jeans despite the weather, who kept shooting sidelong glances Jack's way. The man certainly didn't look familiar. Jack would've remembered the full-sleeve tattoos on each arm, one apparently illustrating the Biblical account of creation and the other depicting the Day of Judgment.

"Who's that guy with the sheriff?" he asked Vera Lynn after they walked away.

"That's his brother Waylon." She sighed. "He... he's been making it known that he'd like to go to the state convention as a delegate."

"Really."

"I'm sure it's just 'cause there's a NASCAR race up the Motor Speedway that weekend. He figures he can get a free room out of it. But he's about as political-minded as a bag of rocks, so I ain't too worried." Still, Jack got the sense that she was downplaying her concern, and that an opponent with connections to the sheriff might be enough to derail his plans.

Dottie Jenkins approached, out of breath, and ushered Jack away to an enclosed tent that was set apart from the cook-off contestants. The other four "secret" judges were already there, each at a table with a dozen small bowls on front of them. He recognized three of them by face, but didn't know their names. The fourth was Waylon Sempel, the Sheriff's brother. Jack sat at the only empty table, which was next to Waylon.

An elderly woman at the far end from Jack spoke up. "I think we should all try each entry together at the same time so we can discuss them."

"That sounds like a fine idea, ma'am," Waylon said. It was the first time Jack had heard him speak, and it was a shock: his voice was gentle and smooth, mellifluous and lilting. It was almost musical.

"All right then," the woman said, "let's try number one."

"Aw hell," said the second judge, a middle-aged lawyer that Jack recalled from a billboard on the interstate. "I can tell you who cooked every one of these. We don't need to worry about no numbers."

They tasted the first one, and even Jack knew right away that it was Rutherford's. The turkey was a dead giveaway. Still, what it lacked in body it made up for in heat.

"I mean no disrespect to Rutherford," Waylon said, "but this ain't a bowl of red, so I think we need to count him out first thing."

"I agree," Jack said, perhaps too eagerly. He knew that a

"bowl of red" had a very strict meaning among folks like these, and he wanted them to know that he knew it. There were two key elements that defined a bowl of red: it always contained beef, and it never contained beans. "This is very nice, but no beef has to be a deal-breaker," Jack said. The other judges nodded in assent.

As they went through the next few bowls, Jack and Waylon found themselves agreeing almost aggressively with each other. Each one was attempting to assume the mantle of leadership, but neither was willing to risk dissent.

There was brief discussion over whether or not a chili made with venison qualified as a bowl of red, in light of their earlier stand against non-beef entries. Most everyone seemed to think that it should, but none of the judges liked it enough for the question to become a serious issue.

Jack prepared himself to say something clever about Bill Hibbert's Japanese beef chili, but then discovered that he couldn't identify it among the remaining bowls. His plan was to wait until someone else named the cook, and then offer up some witticism that would endear him to the more rural-minded folk.

But when they took their first bite of bowl number seven, Waylon beat him to the punch: "If this is the best beef they got in Japan," he said, "I think I'm gonna scratch Tokyo off my bucket list." The other judges laughed and agreed.

Waylon was so amiable and engaging, in fact, that Jack began to wonder if he'd just imagined the hostile looks. But when they got to bowl ten—Shelley Hawkins's entry—his doubts went away.

"Do y'all taste that?" Jack asked as he had his first bite, lay-ing on the rural diction just a little too thick. He was trying to plant an idea in their minds before they could form their own opinions about the chili. Since he didn't know why Shelley should be kept out of the running, he had to just make something up. "Kind of tastes a little... metallic or something. Like maybe canned tomatoes? I don't know."

Before anyone else could respond, Waylon shot him the same cold look Jack had seen earlier. "Tastes fine to me," he said. "In fact, I think I'd call this the best of the bunch."

The other judges did not hesitate to join in Waylon's praise. The worst part was that Jack actually agreed with them: the chili was fantastic. If not the best, then at least in the top three. It was thick and aromatic, and seemed to wrap itself around him like a quilt as he cradled the bowl. When he took a spoonful in his mouth, the punch of flavor was immediate but the heat came slow and steady, building even after he swallowed. By the time he got to the next bite, it had burned off just enough that he could keep going without having to stop for a drink of water. It was the only bowl he emptied.

The last two entries were mediocre, perhaps simply because they had the misfortune of following Shelley's masterwork. "Would y'all mind if we settled on first place for Shelley, and then we can talk about second and third?" Waylon asked.

The other judges nodded enthusiastically, and then Waylon turned to Jack, waiting for an answer. "I have to agree it's damn good," Jack said. "There's just something..." As he looked into the faces of the three other judges, he knew that there was no way he could change anyone's mind. Vera Lynn would just have to understand. "Ah, what the hell. First place for Shelley."

Waylon nodded smugly. "All right then," he said, and let his gaze linger on Jack long enough to suggest another message lurking beneath his words: *mess with me, and I will win.*

When Jack came out of the tent, Vera Lynn was waiting for him. "How'd it go?"

"I feel like I just lost a contest I didn't even enter."

"So who won?"

Jack sighed. "Shelley Hawkins." Vera Lynn's face pinched up. "We had to pick her," he said. "She had the best chili."

"Of course she did," Vera Lynn said. "She stole it from Maggie Landreau."

"As in, physically removed it from her possession?"

"You know what I mean. Stole her recipe. I know it takes some skill to cook it, but Maggie's recipe was damn near chef-proof. And it had two very distinct secret ingredients that won her blue ribbons in about a dozen different cook-offs."

"So why didn't Maggie Landreau just enter herself?"

"She moved back to Huntsville this past summer. Shelley was caught using Maggie's recipe about five years ago at the fair, but she played it off like it was coincidence. Of course, what with Shelley being best friends with the sheriff's wife, nobody ever did a thing about it. Plus, even with the same recipe, Maggie still beat the pants off her."

"The sheriff's wife," Jack repeated. Now it all made sense. Waylon wasn't just trying to assert his dominance over Jack—he was there to make sure Shelley won. "Isn't it a little suspicious that the sheriff's brother is one of the judges then? Seems like a conflict of interest."

"Everybody knows everybody here," Vera Lynn said. "Of course people are gonna do for each other, just like I'm stumping for you. That ain't a conspiracy, that's just how things are. But stealing recipes, that's a whole other thing."

"How do you know she stole it again?"

"I tasted it, for one thing. But even before that, I saw her at the market on Wednesday buying her ingredients. And she had exactly two things in her cart that no other chili cook in town would possibly get, except for Maggie when she still lived here."

"What were they?"

"I promised Maggie I wouldn't tell nobody her recipe, especially after it got stolen once. But you ain't much of a cook, so I'll tell you one of the secret ingredients." She leaned in closer. "Cocoa powder," she whispered.

"That sounds terrible."

"So terrible you picked it to win," she said.

At the other end of the procession of booths, Dottie was announcing the winners of the cook-off. Sheriff Sempel patted Waylon on the back as Shelley held up her blue ribbon.

Jack turned to Vera Lynn. "Things just got a little harder for me, didn't they?"

10

THE CAPITOL EXTENSION was a massive underground complex just north of the main Capitol building in downtown Austin; at ground level, the only evidence of its existence were the long, smoke-tinted skylights hidden behind banks of hedges, and the open-air rotunda that looked like a gigantic wishing well, its interior walls lined with Roman arches all around.

On the second floor, just northeast of the rotunda, Candace found the ornately-framed door for the office of State Representative Donnie Lee Haycombe. He was a white-haired blister of a man with a walrus moustache and a navy suit that was stretched to its limits at every seam.

"Miss Wilder, I appreciate you stopping by while you're in town," Haycombe said. "We're big supporters of the Chamber of Commerce around here. But our session ended six months ago. If there's a bill you're pushing for, I'd suggest coming back next year just before the next session starts."

"The legislative session ended six months ago," she said, "but here you are. Let's just say I'm hopeful the Governor will be calling a special session soon."

"Well, now, that's entirely within the realm of possibility," he said. "But that's his call, and we can only address issues that he personally brings to us."

"And that's why I'd like you to recommend to the Governor that now is the right time to pass a law guaranteeing the right to secret-ballot voting."

His white moustache pulled back like drapes as he smiled. "I'm flattered you think I have that kind of influence," he said.

"Representative Haycombe, I live fifteen hundred miles from here, and even I know that you're the worst-kept secret in Texas politics. They call you the Gatekeeper. Not only do you regulate what bills come to the floor, but you control *when* a bill gets a vote—and that can mean everything, can't it?"

"Oh, I wouldn't say that. Bills at the end of session always get a bit more of a pass, if that's what you're talking about. People anxious to get back to their real jobs and families and all. We're all part-timers around here, Miss Wilder, and I'm afraid we're paid like it too."

"I can help with that," she said.

He stared at her and said nothing. His breathing was just loud and strained enough to call attention to it; he sounded as if he had a slow leak. "Just to be clear," he finally said, "the Governor sets his own agenda for special sessions. If he asks for my opinion, I'll gladly give it. So what's this bill you've got?"

Candace pulled out a thin stack of papers. "It guarantees the right to secret-ballot voting whenever people are required to elect representation."

"Since when don't people vote with a secret ballot?" he asked.

"When union officials are trying to unionize businesses, they do public sign-ups with employees. If they get a majority of employees to sign up, then they're unionized. But this means that the pro-union people are free to pressure or browbeat employees into signing up. There's no opportunity for workers to make their choice in private, like with government elections."

Haycombe glanced through the papers. "This already been passed in other states?"

"Four states so far," Candace said. "Same basic wording. We're trying to move fast since we're fighting Congress at the federal level on it. If we wait until after the election, it might be too late."

"I notice this doesn't say anything about union votes," Haycombe said.

"That's right. It just guarantees that any legally required vote for electing representatives be done by secret ballot. It covers unions, but doesn't single them out. Makes a stronger case that we're not going after them specifically."

"Can't say I see a downside," Haycombe said. "But again, it ain't up to me. So if this does come up in special session, how do you see the vote going?"

"That depends," she said. "How many buttons do you plan on pressing?"

His expression turned serious. "I surely don't know what

you're gettin' at," he said.

Candace reached into her pocket and pulled out her phone, tapping away as she spoke. "You know how it is. Sometimes those early morning votes catch your colleagues by surprise, don't they? Might only be a couple dozen people on the floor sometimes. Same with those late-night votes. But thank goodness they've got a friend like you to cover for them."

She held the phone out so Haycombe could see the screen. The video was of him, on the floor of the legislature, probably taken from the upper gallery during session the previous year. He was wearing the same suit. The floor was relatively empty, despite a general air of busyness; only about a third of the state representatives' seats were filled.

In the background, the Speaker could be heard calling for a vote. Haycombe reached to the electronic voting box on his desk and cast a "Yea" vote. Then he leaned across to the empty seat of his deskmate and cast a "Yea" vote there as well. After that, he got up and walked past the empty desks in front and behind his, casting "Yea" votes at every unoccupied seat.

Candace stopped the playback. "For a man your size, Mister Haycombe, you are quite agile. Seven votes in less than a minute. I'm not knocking it; I'd say it's downright industrious of you. Besides, the leadership doesn't sanction anyone for it even though it happens right in front of their faces, so who am I to judge? All I'm interested in is making sure those extra votes swing our way."

"I think we're done here," he said, and hauled his massive frame up from his chair.

Candace stood and turned to walk away, but caught herself. "One other thing I meant to ask. How's the cabin?" she asked.

"What cabin is that?"

"The hunting cabin you were given by Hank Longpre. You know, the guy who invented those toll road sensors that let you automatically charge tolls to your credit card without stopping. Very convenient. I'm sure you remember him, since you were the one that pushed through the approval of his state contract. Must've been worth millions to him."

"I resent the insinuation," he said, though the last word sounded more like "in-sinny-ation."

"I apologize," Candace said. "I wasn't trying to insinuate. I was actually stating quite clearly, in no uncertain terms, that you accepted a bribe. But here's the thing: we don't care. Just like we don't care about the special loan rate you got on your house, or the college scholarship your daughter was given even though her GPA was just under the requirement. We also don't care about the living room set that Bob Sanger gave you after you pushed through a resolution honoring his grandfather's World War II squadron.

"Other people might care about those things. But we're on the same team here. That's why I think you'll agree that this bill strengthens the party position. In fact, I have a feeling you and your colleagues will like it so much, you'll be willing to vote for it again and again."

11

With the successful appearance at the chili cook-off behind them, Vera Lynn pressed Jack to keep himself visible in Nobles. "You have to look like you're back for good," Vera Lynn said. "That's the only way people are gonna trust you."

"Fine," said Jack. "What's next on the agenda, then?"

"Bingo."

On Wednesday evenings, the VFW hall was the hub of Nobles social life. The building was modest from the road, dull with age except for the American flag painted vertically up the middle, which had obviously been recently freshened up. Inside, the hall stretched back from the road for what seemed like miles through the smoky haze that curled up into the rafters. If there was a law against smoking in the hall, Jack didn't see anyone eager to enforce it. Especially Sheriff Hil Sempel, who sat at a table directly in front of the number basket.

And right next to him sat his brother Waylon.

Jack and Vera Lynn checked in at a card table near the front door. The cashier was an ashen-faced lady who took Vera Lynn's "how are you" as an opportunity to launch into a lengthy tale of medical woe. Jack feigned interest, but by the end he couldn't even remember if she was talking about gall stones or kidney stones.

Once her tale was told, Jack handed her a twenty, and she gave him four thick bingo cards. The cards were ancient pressboard topped with a fake wood pattern; they had endured so many years of dirt, stains, and general abuse that they were beginning to resemble actual wood. Each numbered square had a red plastic shutter that could be pulled across it to mark when that number was called. "Some of the shutters are missing," she said. "Just use a peanut if you have to."

As they walked into the main hall, Jack said, "These are literally the same cards they used when we were kids."

"They tried to bring in them paper cards that you dab the ink on as you go," said Vera Lynn, "but too many folks weren't having it. Hell, Nancy's been using the same exact cards for twenty-five years now. She's got them set aside with a rubber band around them with her name on it."

"She must do well with them," said Jack.

"She pretty much never wins with those cards," Vera Lynn said. "But by God, they're hers."

Vera Lynn led Jack to a table immediately behind Sheriff Sempel, and introduced him to a few more people whose names left his head as soon as he heard them. He was too preoccupied with Waylon Sempel, watching the man like a boxer studies his opponent. More than once Waylon glanced back at him, too, and Jack had to shift his gaze away in a hurry.

"So I guess you heard about the state primary," Vera Lynn said, trying to draw his attention back.

"Yeah," said Jack. "Delayed till the end of May."

"This whole damn thing's been knocked off the rails by the new voting maps."

"The redistricting?" he asked. He remembered the map in Emmet Washburn's office, with all the irregular shapes and colors.

"Yep. Now we're part of the Twenty-Fifth, which used to be down south of Austin. Now it goes from us, all the way north to just outside Fort Worth."

"So are they just going to delay the local conventions?"

"They can't. Used to be we'd have a precinct convention on the day of the primary, but that doesn't give enough time before the state convention. So now they're saying we may not have precinct conventions, and the county convention is in April—*before* the primary. So the delegates are picked before they even know who they're supposed to vote for."

"I don't think there's any doubt who's going to win," said Jack.

"Still. Couldn't have a more cattywampus system if they were trying to."

The room was filled by now, and the bingo caller—who, Jack noticed, was the ashen cashier from when they arrived—took the stage.

"First round," she said into a microphone next to the number basket. "In honor of our sheriff, we're playing 'Big H.'" Hil seemed tickled by the tribute, and swigged a beer in his own honor.

"'Big H,' what's that?" asked Jack.

"You got to make an 'H' on one of your cards," Vera Lynn said, sliding the shutters to show him. The B and O columns were filled, along with a horizontal line across the center row. It was like three bingos in one; Jack guessed that it would take a while to turn up a winner.

As the caller started shouting out numbers, Jack was surprised at how hard it was to keep up with just four cards. Several of the bingo veterans around him had six or even eight cards, but every time a number was read, Jack was still searching on his third or fourth card for the previous number.

Once two of his cards started getting close to the Big H, he concentrated on those two and stopped checking the losers. Vera Lynn was focusing on her own cards, and didn't notice how close Jack was to winning.

When the caller said "B-7," Jack shouted "Bingo!" more as an expression of surprise than victory. He slid the shutter across the winning square on his card, and then heard a faint "Bingo" called out across the room. It was Nancy, Jack's tenth-grade English teacher—and, according to Vera Lynn, perennial Wednesday-night bingo loser.

"Take it back," Vera Lynn whispered to Jack.

"Huh?"

"Say you were wrong. Let her win." A checker was squeezing through the tables toward Jack to verify his card.

"But I got bingo."

"Are you here to win bingo, or to become an elector?"

Jack saw her point. How would it look to come in and win right out of the gate, taking half the pot from a lady who's been at it for twenty-five years? As the checker got to his table, Jack took his hand and wiped it across his card, opening all the shutters. "My mistake," he told the checker. "Guess I jumped the gun."

Apparently, Jack discovered, this was one of the biggest blunders a person can make in bingo. The players in the immediate vicinity offered some good-natured ribbing, and he swallowed his pride, knowing it was all for a greater purpose.

Then he heard Sheriff Sempel weigh in, just loud enough for Jack to hear. "Looks like Ray's boy plays bingo the same way his old man counted up votes on election day," he said. "With a few extra thrown in, just in case."

Most of the people at Hil's table laughed raucously, though Waylon just trained his eyes on Jack and let smoke drift out of his mouth like a damp log smoldering on a campfire.

"What's the sheriff's deal?" asked Jack. "Did he hate Dad or something?"

"Daddy helped him get elected," Vera Lynn said. "But I never understood why, because they didn't exactly see eye to eye on much."

"Town not big enough for the both of them, probably," said Jack.

"And there's that other thing," Vera Lynn said.

"What other thing?"

They heard a cheer from the other side of the hall as Nancy's card was verified as a winner. After the clapping and whooping had died down, Vera Lynn leaned in close to Jack.

"Daddy's the one sent Waylon to prison."

12

IT WAS EARLY MORNING on the fourth day of the special legislative session that the voter privacy bill finally came up for a vote. Candace had spent most of the previous three days and nights at the Capitol, camped out in the House chamber gallery as dozens of other bills whizzed by on their way to becoming either full-fledged laws or quickly-forgotten footnotes in the legislative record.

The chamber would ebb and flow with representatives, very few of whom appeared to be paying much attention at all to the bills being read. Small groups of legislators carried on their own discussions, most of which danced along with the easy rhythms of small talk rather than state business. Then, when it was time to vote, they would stop mid-sentence, hurry off to their desks to press their voting buttons, and then return to their conversations.

On that morning of the fourth day, the room was especially light on legislators; a local restaurant owner had set up a buffet table on the lawn outside the Capitol, and was preparing breakfast burritos as a thank-you to the representatives for their hard work. Even the normal crowd milling about the Chamber floor had been drawn outside, leaving only about a dozen legislators inside.

As soon as the room cleared, Candace saw Representative Haycombe signal to the Speaker, and the voting privacy bill was pulled from the bottom of a stack of papers in the Speaker's hands. He quickly read through the bill, which had been carefully whittled down to two sentences that would guarantee a Texas voter's right to vote by secret ballot. When the call for vote came, Haycombe and his cohorts spread out and went from table to table, pushing "Yea" votes at every station. From what Candace could tell, there was one lone Democrat who was trying to counter the vote by scrambling to the unoccupied stations near her and pressing "Nay."

The vote was not even close.

*   *   *

Candace returned to the Nexus and gave the team the news. "Platt's breakfast plan paid off," she said.

Langhorne went to one of the four whiteboards that dominated the walls of the main work room and put a green checkmark next to a line that read "Voter Privacy Act." To no one in particular, he offered a distracted "Good work."

Miles glanced around at the boards, all filled to capacity with similar lines of text that outlined every step of their plan. "One down," he said, "five hundred to go."

"Now it's time to move on some of our solid targets," Langhorne said. "Who do we have?"

Fleming stood to speak, a habit that gave her the air of a military officer. "So far, we only have six that seem like shoo-ins for elector slots. The good news is that two of them are Sleeping Dogs."

"What does that mean?" asked Platt.

Fleming opened her mouth to answer, but Candace cut in. "Sleeping Dogs are former Democrats that switched over to the Republican Party about ten years ago, as part of a plan to keep tabs on the other side. You've heard of Blue Dogs?"

Platt nodded. "Conservative Democrats," he said. "More in the Old South tradition."

"Exactly. Seems hard to believe now, but Democrats dominated the Texas House and Senate up until 1996. In fact, in 1958, under a Republican president, there were exactly zero Republicans elected to the Texas legislature."

"But in the late Nineties," Fleming said, "a lot of Texas Democrats started to jump ship. The whole country was tilting to the right, and Republicans were branding themselves as the party of family values, so it was an easy move for some of them."

"But not all," Candace cut in again. "Some families had been voting Democrat for generations. And they still supported laws to protect small farmers and laborers instead of big businesses. So a small group of high-level Democratic Party members came up with a plan: they would publicly defect to the Republican Party, but privately they'd remain loyal to the Democrats. They called themselves the Sleeping Dogs, and they've been feeding us inside info ever since."

"So you're saying we can count on these two Sleeping Dogs for sure," Platt said.

"It's about as certain as anything can be with this plan," Fleming answered.

"What about the other four?" asked Langhorne.

"That would depend on what we can turn up on them. We get something good, we might be able to shake them loose."

"So what if," said Miles, "instead of waiting to see who gets picked as electors, we try to push some ringers through?"

"There's no way we're going to just sneak electors into the college," Candace said. "These have to be people with long-term connections to the party. Even then, we can't have them pursue it too aggressively or we'll risk suspicion."

"We could try some chaff deployment," Platt said.

"Some what?" asked Miles.

"Chaff. Pilots in World War Two used it to avoid being detected by radar. They had small tubes filled with aluminum strips that they'd release into the air, and the strips would cause radar signals to go crazy. A radar operator couldn't tell the plane from the chaff, so they couldn't target it."

"In other words," Langhorne said, "we hide our electors in plain sight, by surrounding them with..."

"Chaff," Platt said.

"Chaff," Langhorne repeated, and smiled.

13

"So you're a registered Republican?" Silas asked.

Jack nodded, mouth full. They were eating lunch at the office instead of heading down the street to Güero's or Magnolia Cafe—part of Jack's plan to reduce spending until he could sign some more clients. The lunch was from ThunderCloud Subs, a locally famous chain with a location just one block from the office. Jack: Traditional Club. Silas: Roast Beef & Avocado. Marlene: Veggie Delite with hummus and sprouts.

"I've known you for what, almost twenty years?" Silas said. "You've always avoided talking about politics. I don't think you ever mentioned that you're registered to vote, even."

"I was still living at home at the time. My dad was a Republican Party official. It wasn't exactly what I'd call a choice."

"So you're not *really* Republican."

Jack shrugged. "I think the government spends way too much money and makes it hard as hell to run a small business," he said. "But I also don't give a rat's ass if two gay guys want to get married. So what does that make me?"

"Normal," Marlene said.

"So where's that party? The normal party?"

"Anybody who's paid attention at all for the past thirty years can tell you," Silas said, "that both the major parties suck. They just suck in different ways. You wanna know the difference between Democrats and Republicans? Democrats have all these idealistic goals like ending poverty, improving education, and saving the environment, but then they either don't do anything, or they institute moronic policies that cause all sorts of unintended pain for the very people they're trying to help. Republicans, on the other hand, well… they cause exactly the pain they intend to cause."

"What are you then?" Marlene asked Silas through a mouthful of sandwich, a sprig of sprouts dangling from her lip. "Libertarian? Like Roark Bennett?"

"Hell no," he said. "I live in the real world. Libertarians tend to have this child-like view that corporations will behave sensibly and in the best interest of everyone, even though that has never once happened in the history of the free market. You're better off believing in the power of fairy dust."

"What does that leave?" asked Marlene.

"Like Jack was saying, there's just no place in our current political framework for common freaking sense. And that makes me a sad polar bear." Silas held up a stuffed bear that Polar Air had sent to the office, dabbed its furry paws to its eyes, and made sobbing sounds.

"Stop," Marlene said, and grabbed the stuffed bear. "You're getting avocado on Sherman."

"Back on topic," Jack said. "What should I do about this Waylon guy?"

"What's there to do?" asked Silas. "You didn't send him to jail."

"I know, I just... I don't want him to..."

"Beat your ass?" Marlene offered.

"Yeah. Kinda."

"Then be the bigger man," she said. "Treat him with respect, and he'll be forced to do the same."

Jack was impressed. "That's actually some sound advice. Thanks, Marlene."

"You're welcome. But also, carry a knife in your back pocket, just in case."

14

CANDACE HEADED NORTH from the Nexus to Martin Luther King Jr. Boulevard, and then went west. This was the neighborhood between the Capitol and the University of Texas; as she turned north on Guadalupe, the formality of state buildings gave way to the funkiness of local business. She parked in front of a narrow, nondescript storefront wedged between a vegetarian restaurant and a vintage clothing shop.

Inside, a dozen people—nearly all of whom appeared to be college students—bustled about, some earnestly pleading into phone receivers and others scribbling frenetically on whiteboards. Posters and signs that read "Roark Bennett for President" were tacked up in any unused space. On the door to a small office in back was taped a sheet of paper with two words written in black Sharpie: "Galt's Gulch."

Candace knocked and was invited in. A small, silver-haired man in a striped polo stood up behind the desk. "Congressman Bennett, it's a pleasure," Candace said, shaking his hand.

"Call me Roark," he said. "And that's my manager Harry lurking behind you. Don't mind him. He sits in on just about everything."

Candace turned and nodded at an ashen man in dress shirt and tie who seemed to disappear into the wall even as she looked.

"I understand you've got quite the track record with smaller races on both sides of the aisle," Bennett said.

"Thanks. But I came here to talk about you."

He leaned back in his leather executive chair, which only accentuated his frail, hunched frame; he almost appeared to be slipping slowly under his desk. "I'm listening," he said.

"You enjoy the support of a very passionate base," she said. "There's no doubt at all about that. But making that jump from popular fringe candidate to broad support from the Republican Party has been... challenging."

"They hate me," Bennett said. "I don't fall in line when they snap their fingers."

"I admire that," she said. "But frankly, that strategy is never going to earn you the nomination."

"That's why we're going straight to the people," he said. "Once we get our message out, they'll be forced to give us the nomination because the people will demand it."

"Here's your problem: you can't turn that many people in such a short amount of time. It's not possible. Look at your campaign posters." Candace pointed to one on the wall. "It says Roark Bennett for President because if it didn't, most voters would have no idea what you were running for."

"I hope you didn't come all the way down here just to tell

me I'm going to lose, because—and try not to be shocked—you're not the first person to make that prediction."

"I didn't come here for that," she said. "You *are* going to lose. But I'm here to tell you how you can still get the thing you want most."

"You just said I wasn't going to get the nomination."

"But that's not what you're really after, is it? That's just a way to get the thing you want."

"Which is?"

"Influence over the party platform. Real discussion about the issues everyone else is afraid to talk about."

Bennett cocked his head, considering her words. "Fair enough," he said. "So how do I get that without getting the nomination?"

"You need delegates. But not enough to win... just enough to keep Randell from winning on the first ballot at the national convention."

"How do you propose getting delegates if I can't win the popular vote in a primary?"

"All you have to do is play by the rules," Candace said. "Take advantage of the way the caucus system is set up to strategically position your supporters."

"Take advantage how?"

"The national delegates are selected from pools of state delegates. State delegates are chosen from county delegates, which are chosen from precinct delegates. Which means you have to stack the delegate rosters with your supporters as early as possible, at the precinct and county conventions."

Harry, Bennett's campaign manager, peeled himself from the background. "But if the majority of people support Randell in the primary," he said, "then Randell will get the delegates."

"Really?" Candace asked. "Who chooses the delegates?"

"The people at the convention," Harry said.

"Which doesn't necessarily have anything to do with who voters choose in the primary. Especially since Texas isn't even going to have a primary until *after* the local conventions. The delegates are chosen by the handful of people stubborn and/or dedicated enough to stick around after the other convention business is done. If you can get your supporters to stick around after most everyone else goes home, then it doesn't matter who everyone else supports. Once the Bennett people make up a majority of the attendees, they can set the agenda and choose the delegates to send on to the next higher level."

"So Randell wins the primary on paper," Harry said, "but our supporters are the ones chosen as delegates."

"Right. And if your delegates campaign hard at the state convention for national delegate slots, then those delegates will have a direct influence over who gets the nomination."

"And that," Bennett said, "is what gets me a seat at the table."

"Exactly," said Candace.

Bennett smiled and narrowed his eyes. "What's in this for you?" he asked.

"Consider me a fan," she said. "I'm sick of the same old two-party gridlock that never accomplishes anything. Also, I'm working with the Chamber of Commerce now. We think you could use this opportunity to push through some serious pro-business strategies."

"Like muzzling the EPA," he said. "And getting rid of the

federal minimum wage."

"Randell's too moderate to campaign on those issues. But what if you could secure a place in his administration, in exchange for your delegates? Then you could work from the inside."

"So you're saying I should get them to put me in charge of a department that I don't think should exist in the first place," he said, laughing.

"Can you think of a better way to defang big government?"

"Young lady, I like the way you think."

She pulled a thick file from her bag and laid it on his desk. "This is an action plan to help mobilize your supporters before the local conventions. You don't have a lot of time."

Bennett waved Harry over and handed him the file. "Don't worry about that," Bennett told her. "Our people are like the Minutemen. Bennett's Brigade, ready at a moment's notice."

15

On the morning of the county convention, fresh out of the shower, Jack stood in front of the bathroom mirror and practiced his speech. He knew there would be people at the county convention that didn't know him, and might not even know of his father. He needed to get his pitch down cold if he wanted them to choose him as a state delegate.

The phone rang, and Jack saw that it was Vera Lynn. He picked up. "I was just going through my speech," he said.

Vera Lynn sounded as if she'd just run from the other side of town. "Jack, you better get down here."

"Why? What's going on?"

"The precinct convention," she said, pausing to catch her breath. "They're having it now... without you."

*   *   *

The Nobles County Courthouse was a Romanesque Victorian beast hewn from blocks of yellow granite, embedded into the center of the town square as if it had erupted there. Its rough-surfaced walls were balanced by smooth columns with delicately ornate plinths and capitals. At the front rose a clock tower, visible from almost anywhere in town. On the open grass lawn that surrounded it stood a century-old granite monument engraved "To Our Confederate Dead."

When Jack pulled up to the courthouse, Vera Lynn was already inside arguing with Dottie Jenkins. He couldn't make out words, but he had been yelled at enough by his sister over the years to recognize her voice before he even saw her.

As he opened the door, his sister's words suddenly clarified: "Bullcrap and you know it, Dottie!"

"We did exactly what we were supposed to," Dottie said. "If you can't be troubled to read the postings at City Hall-"

"-tacked up on a cork board behind the security desk. Ain't nobody ever looked at that board and you know it."

Dottie saw Jack and lowered her voice. "This is a strange year for everybody, what with the primary being delayed. I'm doing the best I can. We didn't even know we were having a precinct convention until two weeks ago."

Vera Lynn motioned to the small crowd of Republican Party members gathered in the courthouse foyer. "Looks like you managed to tell *some* people," she said.

Jack touched Vera Lynn's shoulder. "It's fine," he said. "I'm here. We've still got time, right?"

Dottie flashed a weary smile. "Vera Lynn's been keeping us occupied. Jack, I'm gonna need to see your voter registration card."

Jack pulled the card, soft with age, from his wallet and handed it to her. "All right then," she said, but didn't look up as she handed it back.

"Think we got a problem here," a bellowing voice said, and Jack turned to see Sheriff Sempel.

"What problem is that, Hil?" Vera Lynn asked, planting her hands on her hips. She was not one for formal pleasantries even under ideal circumstances; with the mood she was in, Jack feared she might get herself arrested.

"There's a certain issue of residency," Sempel said. "No offense to you, Jack, but you don't live in this precinct anymore."

"But this is where I'm registered," Jack said. "This is where the Travis County Chair told me I should come."

"I think he might have been trying to kick the can outta his own yard and into our yard." Sempel paused, then added somberly: "You're the can in this scenario."

"What a crock of crap," Vera Lynn said, and stormed out of the building, cursing incoherently.

"So that's it?" Jack asked. "Can't I plead my case to someone? It doesn't seem fair since I was doing what I was told I should do."

"Rules are rules," Dottie said, though her expression was apologetic. "I'm sorry, Jack."

Jack's brain was spinning, trying to latch onto any obscure tidbit from the Party Handbook that might turn the situation back in his favor. "But I'm still part of the same district, right?" he asked. "So the other precincts are meeting here before the county convention too, right? I can just join with whatever precinct I'm supposed to be with."

Dottie shook her head. "It goes by county, not by Congressional district. And Austin is in a different county."

Jack couldn't help but wonder why someone hadn't said something sooner. After all, just about everyone in town knew his plan. Was it all part of Sheriff Sempel's strategy to take him out of the running?

Jack looked around for his sister. Where had she gone? At the far end of the foyer, waiting for the convention to start, was Waylon Sempel, dressed in a plain dark suit and tie with a white dress shirt. Jack's father would have called them "church clothes," but in the case of Waylon, Jack guessed that they could probably be more accurately described as his "court clothes." Not that it mattered; Waylon and Hil had obviously won.

But Jack remembered what Marlene had said, and realized that the advice was even more relevant now. It was easy to be a gracious winner; the challenge was losing like a man. He walked over to Waylon and held out his hand. "Good luck," he said. "I hope you make it to the state convention."

Waylon stared at Jack's hand with suspicion, but eventually took it in his own and shook. He didn't speak, but gave a slight nod. Jack felt like something had thawed between them. Even if his whole elector plan was shot, at least there was something good that came out of it. And maybe he would look back on all this as groundwork for becoming an elector next time.

Vera Lynn came running back into the courthouse waving a sheet of paper. She held it up and read it, the words crammed between labored breaths. "For and in consideration of the sum of one dollar, I, Vera Lynn Patton, hereby quit-claim to John Arthur Patton all right, title, and interest in and to the real property situated in Nobles County, Texas, and described as an 1886 Victorian two-story family dwelling situated on .36 acres located at 711 Main Street."

Jack just stood slack jawed, in awe of his sister's cleverness. She turned to him and whispered, "You got a dollar?"

Jack dug for his wallet and pulled out a single bill. He held it up for the people gathered around to see, and presented it with a theatrical flourish to his sister.

"Brenda, get over here," Vera Lynn called out to someone in the crowd. A possum-faced woman in an American flag t-shirt poked through. "Would you mind notarizing this for us?" Vera Lynn asked.

"I'd be happy to," Brenda said, and turned her head from the sheriff as she passed.

All parties signed the deed, and Vera Lynn offered it to Dottie. "I believe you'll find that my brother is now exactly where he's supposed to be," she said.

Dottie looked to the sheriff, then back to the deed. She threw her hands into the air. "I guess that's that," she said. "Enjoy the convention, Jack."

As Jack and Vera Lynn headed toward the meeting hall, Sheriff Sempel let out a heavy sigh, then cleared the way.

"Some sister you got," Sempel said as Jack passed.

The precinct convention was a small affair, with just a dozen or so participants. Jack realized that the gathering crowd at the courthouse was for the other precincts and the county convention that would follow. Stacks of candidate signs were piled high on tables throughout the room. The largest stacks were for Governor James Randell of Florida. Dottie began the convention by leading the group in the Pledge of Allegiance, which was followed by a short prayer.

"Looks like we better get to it before we're crowded out of the room," Dottie said. "We've got three precinct delegate slots open, and I've got three names on the roster for approval. Those are Waylon Sempel, Bill Hibbert, and Jack Patton. Can we get a vote on those? Just raise your hand for a yes."

Jack looked around and saw all hands go up. He felt a sudden rush.

"All right then," Dottie said. "That's that. But we still need three alternates. Anybody want to volunteer?" All hands went down. "We can't finish the meeting till we name some alternates," she said.

"Does it mean we'll be stuck here all afternoon?" Brenda asked.

"It just might," Dottie said, and the rest of the group let out a collective groan. Still, Brenda raised her hand to volunteer, as did the chili thief, Shelley Hawkins. "Just one more," said Dottie.

"I'll do it," Vera Lynn said, with a tone that expressed a desire to end the meeting more than a desire to participate in the political process.

"Oh, I don't know if you're eligible, hon," Dottie said with a wink. "I heard you just sold your house."

*   *   *

Jack and the other delegates waited outside so the other precincts could use the courthouse space for their own conventions. As the starting time of the county convention approached, the crowds at the courthouse continued to grow larger and more restless. The majority of the new arrivals carried signs for Roark Bennett. It seemed to Jack a foregone conclusion that Randell would be the Republican nominee, but Bennett's followers seemed dedicated, bordering on fanatical.

"Didn't know Bennett was a contender," Jack said.

"He's not," said Vera Lynn. "But it looks like they're gonna try and take over the convention anyway."

Vera Lynn squeezed through the crowd and waved down someone Jack couldn't see. She came back a few minutes later. "You gotta get in there and get your name on the list," she said. "The County Chair is in there making a slate for Randell supporters so they can just vote to approve the whole slate at once. But there's only gonna be five delegates and five alternates, so you gotta hurry."

"They're not picking individual delegates?" Jack felt confident that his unique story would be his ticket to getting selected. If they just voted a whole slate of delegates, he would never have a fair shot at winning the vote. Instead, the slots would go to the candidates who happened to get their names on the list first.

"They're trying to keep the Bennett folks from getting their own delegates in, which would kill your chances for sure."

Jack raised up onto the tips of his toes and looked out across the crowd. The people were shoving and shouting, trying to force themselves through the only open doorway of the courthouse. Sheriff Sempel was trapped somewhere inside, and his deputies stood outside the building with no clue how to handle the situation on their own; they were supposed to help restrict the entrants to delegates only, but Jack could tell that there were far too many people for everyone to be a legitimate delegate.

He fought his way through to the deputy at the top of the stairs, young, flush-faced, and covered in sweat. "Excuse me, sir, but I'm supposed to be in there. I'm one of the delegates."

"Can't let nobody in," the deputy said. "We're already over the fire code limit."

"But by law I have to be allowed in for the convention."

"By law, I *can't* let you in. And I got the badge, so I'm pretty sure I win."

Defeated, Jack stepped back and circled around the side of the courthouse, trying to find another way in. Sitting on the side steps, smoking a cigarette, was Waylon. "Some kinda zoo over there, ain't it?" he said.

"Yeah," Jack answered, pleasantly surprised at Waylon's friendly tone. He felt obligated to keep the conversation going. "I feel bad for your brother."

"He can handle it." Waylon took a long, loving drag on his cigarette. "Y'know, whatever beef my brother had with your old man, I ain't been a part of it. I done what I done, and I paid for it. And it don't matter to me who gets picked for this thing, long as I get to go to Fort Worth."

Jack nodded. It was such a relief for the tension between them to be eased, if not gone completely. "But right now it doesn't look like either of us are going to state. Not unless we can figure out how to get inside and get our names on that slate."

Jack tried the side door, knowing it would be locked. Then he stepped back and looked up at the stone face of the building. "You see that ledge?" he asked, pointing. It was a narrow stone balcony in front of a tall window on the second floor, wide enough for a person to stand but not much else—clearly meant for decoration.

Waylon took one last drag, then stood up and dusted off the seat of his pants. He cupped his hand over his eyes to block the sun as he looked up. "Yep," he said.

"I think the window behind it is open a little bit."

"Looks to be," Waylon said.

"If we could get up there, we could probably get in. Maybe with a ladder."

"Nah. People'd see." Waylon took off his suit jacket and draped it over the metal handrail next to the steps. "Give me a boost," he said.

"Hold on," Jack said. "Before we do this... do you think this is considered breaking into a government building?"

"How's it breaking in if we're supposed to be in there?"

Jack couldn't deny the power of the argument. And the fact that Waylon would be the one taking the risk didn't hurt, either. The swell of noise inside the courthouse surely meant that time was running out, so they had to do something quick.

"Okay then," Jack said, "if you get inside, come back down and unlock this door so I can get in too." He laced his fingers together and held them out for Waylon to step up.

"Yep," Waylon said. With Jack's help, he launched himself up to the balcony and climbed over with the ease of a child on monkey bars at the park. Waylon slid the window open wide and disappeared inside. Jack waited. It was too dark to see inside through the glass-paneled side door, but he didn't take his eyes off it, expecting at any moment that it would burst open.

The noise inside subsided for a while, then erupted anew with even greater volume. After nearly ten minutes of waiting, Jack concluded that Waylon wasn't coming for him. He went back around to the front of the building and found Vera Lynn talking with Brenda, who was a disheveled mess. "Were you inside?" he asked Brenda.

"Only just," she said. "Those Bennett folks are crazy. They were trying to suspend the rules and elect a new Chair so they could give themselves all the state delegate slots. Then the County Chair said the delegates were already picked, and boy, they went *nuts*. I figured I should get out before things got ugly. They never even said who the state delegates are."

"So it's done?" Jack asked.

Brenda nodded. "Sorry, Jack. I don't know how they can call that a real convention though. You'd think someone would make 'em do it again and follow the rules next time."

It wasn't long before Sheriff Sempel forced his way through the crowd with two men in handcuffs, passed them off to his deputies, and went back in for more.

Jack kept watching the entrance for Waylon. He would have to come out eventually, and Jack planned on being there when he did. He wanted an explanation.

After Sheriff Sempel brought out two more people in handcuffs, the crowd of Bennett supporters began to disperse, enthusiastically chanting slogans as they went. Finally Waylon appeared, chatting and laughing with a woman holding a Randell campaign sign.

"What happened?" Jack asked as he approached.

"Oh yeah," Waylon said, as if he had completely forgotten about Jack until that very moment. "Turns out that door's wired to an alarm. Couldn't open it. Too bad, huh?"

"That's it?" asked Jack. "That's your excuse?"

"Don't look so pissed off," Waylon said. "I got us picked."

"You did? How?"

"Just had to give 'em our names and they put us on the slate. Then they rammed it through without a full vote, so the Bennett folks totally crapped their pants about it. But hey... whatever gets it done." Waylon handed Jack a copy of the delegate list.

Jack saw Waylon's name in the delegate column, but not his own. Then he glanced over to the other column. "I'm an alternate," he said.

"That was all they had left," Waylon said. "Who cares? We're all goin' to Fort Worth either way."

"*I* care. If I'm only an alternate, I can't get picked as an elector."

"Look, man, it was crazy in there. I did what I could. Just be glad you got that." Waylon walked off, and spat on the pavement as he went.

Jack thought about the obstacles that had piled up against him every single step of the way in his quest to become an elector. In a sadistic way, it was almost funny. But he wasn't out of the running yet. If there was a way to get himself a position as a full-fledged state delegate, he'd find it.

16

Candace scrolled through video highlights of the chaos at county conventions across the state. "Bennett's people are exceeding expectations," she said. "The county chairs were so desperate to keep Bennett's Brigade off the slate that they approved just about anyone with a Randell button and a heartbeat. Half of our ringers made it to the state convention as primaries or alternates."

"Good start," Langhorne said. "We'll see if it pays off. Where are we on the other four shoo-ins?"

Grant opened a folder. "Not a whole lot on them yet. One is definitely cheating on his wife, and another one probably is, but we don't have pictures or video. We do have one who's in some serious debt. Nolan Robeson. Upside-down on his house, and his business is going under with a huge outstanding loan."

"Maybe try the financial incentive angle?" Candace offered.

"Make sure the bank's really putting the screws to him first," Langhorne said. "And have somebody call his house while he's gone. Pretend to be from a collection agency. Get his wife worried."

"We should *Godfather* him," Miles said.

A room full of puzzled faces stared back in silence.

"You know... the guy needs help, right? So we offer him the money now as a favor, but don't tell him what we want just yet. Say we'll expect a favor in return sometime in the future. Then the money's all gone by the time he finds out what we want, so he can't back out."

Candace said, "Sounds like you've got some experience with this."

"Sure," said Miles. "I've seen it like twelve times."

"Okay then, Miles," Langhorne said, "this one's yours. Fleming, lock in the Sleeping Dogs but don't give them the details yet."

Miles raised a hand. "Wait a second. You're talking about me actually doing this? I thought that's what he was for." He nodded toward Vig. "I'm pretty sure this guy could beat me up with just his neck muscles."

Vig said nothing.

"We're all going to get our hands dirty at some point," Langhorne said.

"But... I really don't know anything about... anything. I just watch a lot of movies. I've never intimidated or threatened someone. I get anxiety nosebleeds, for God's sake."

Langhorne pulled a sheet from Grant's folder and laid it gently in front of Miles. "You'll figure it out. Now what about that fourth shoo-in, Grant?"

Grant shook his head. "George Vestry. No secret vices, no leverage. Nothing. I can't see us swaying him."

Langhorne looked at the file. "So many things can happen between now and then. We'll just have to wait and see."

＊   ＊   ＊

Miles and Vig made the trip to see Nolan Robeson in Sugar Land, a world unto itself on the western edge of Houston. His home was not one of the cookie-cutter models jammed together along the shores of Venetian Lake, but a spacious estate on the richer side of Cleveland Lake. It had the look of a Mediterranean villa, complete with a decorative campanile and tall Palladian windows.

Robeson was all leathery tan, bright white smile, and little else. "So I hear you boys are investors?" he said, popping open a Rio Blanco Pale Ale and collapsing into a leather recliner. He did not offer anything to his guests, but motioned for them to sit.

"We are," Miles said, "of a sort. We're interested in making an investment... in you."

"My custom Jacuzzi business, you mean."

"No. You, personally."

Robeson sized them up. "What exactly is it you're looking for?"

"The question is, what are *you* looking for? Judging by your company's sales reports for the last few months, I'd say cash is what you need."

Robeson's white smile shifted, and looked more like a snarl.

"This is a fantastic place you got here," Miles continued,

glancing around. "I assume Mrs. Robeson doesn't know about the Notice of Default yet."

"Who the hell you think you are?" Robeson said.

"Allies," Miles said. "Benefactors. We want to help you get through this."

Vig handed Miles a briefcase, and Miles laid it flat on Robeson's glass coffee table. He opened it, revealing the stacks of cash inside.

Robeson dragged his tongue around his lips, lost in thought as he stared at the money.

"Go ahead," Miles said. "It's yours."

Robeson touched the stack of bills, flipped through the corners to ensure that they were all real. "What's the catch?" he asked without looking up.

"You strike us as someone who likes money," Miles said. "And as someone who might be able to help us out one day."

"Is this dirty?" Robeson asked. "You boys trying to set me up?"

"One hundred percent clean."

Robeson's voice lowered. "You expect me to kill somebody?"

Miles shook his head, confused. "No, no, nothing like that. Whatever we ask of you, I promise it will be legal and will not involve hurting anyone."

"Oh," Robeson said, and sounded a bit disappointed. "All right then. See yourselves out." He closed the briefcase, placed it next to his recliner, and used his remote to turn on the TV.

Miles was taken aback. "We'll... be in touch," he said, and they left.

Once they were outside, Miles turned to Vig. "How'd I

do? You think I sold it?"

Vig stayed silent until they were inside the car. "You shouldn't have given him all of it at once," he said.

"I shouldn't? How was I supposed to know that? I haven't done this before." Miles ran his hands nervously through his long hair. "How much was in there?"

"Five hundred thousand," Vig said.

"Whoa. That ought to keep him flush for a while."

Vig checked the rear view mirror and pulled out of the driveway. "He'll be broke again in a month," he said.

17

The Credentials Committee meeting was held the morning before the state convention began, which meant that Jack could beat the rush into Fort Worth—or so he thought. Silas had warned him against trying to drive into town. "You might as well just park in Burleson and start walking," he said, "because it's gonna be quicker than sitting on I-35." But it was such a nice straight shot north from Austin, and Jack found himself longing for the wide-open spaces north of Waco in towns like Grandview and Hillsboro. That, coupled with the fact that he was going early, convinced him that driving wouldn't be so bad.

He was wrong.

Cars were lined up for miles as thousands of politicians, delegates, and guests descended upon the city. It was nearly midnight by the time he made it to his hotel; instead of having a nice dinner and going on a walking tour of the area, he ate a candy bar from the room's mini-fridge and then fell asleep with the TV on.

The next morning, on his short walk to the convention, he finally got to see a bit of the city. From the front entrance on Houston Street, the Fort Worth Convention Center looked more like some kind of endless New York brownstone than an exhibition hall. Even in downtown Austin, Jack never felt like he was walking through manmade canyons the way he did here. And looking out from the Eleventh Street entrance, down a narrow road bordered by stone and steel giants made all the more monstrous by their blandness, Saint Patrick Cathedral stood perfectly framed, a squat, wart-covered relic that looked like it was built by children armed with fistfuls of white clay mud after a storm. It was achingly beautiful.

Inside the convention center, there was clearly still work to be done; tables were still being set up, and handmade signs filled the void until professional signage could be properly installed. Jack found his way to a large meeting room marked with a sheet of paper that said "Credentials Committee."

Judging by the size of the crowd in the room, there were a lot of credentials challenges to go through. Jack had no idea if Waylon was supposed to be there or not—since it was his credentials that Jack was challenging—but there was no sign of him.

As the meeting wore on, the pattern of challenges became clear: Bennett supporters were complaining that they had been unfairly excluded from delegate slates all across the state, due to claims that they were not qualified to serve as delegates. On the flipside, a handful of Randell supporters claimed that Bennett's Brigade had overtaken their local conventions and pushed through their own people even though the Randell people held a majority. To a person, their challenges were struck down, under the argument that the selected delegates all had valid credentials, and the question of how they were chosen was not an issue for the Credentials Committee to decide.

When it finally came time for Jack's challenge, he walked to the podium in the center aisle of the room. The chair of the committee read from the file in the dull, weary voice of a man with a full day's worth of complaints still ahead of him.

"This is a challenge to the credentials of Waylon Sempel, delegate for the Twenty-Fifth District. States that Mister Sempel is on probation and therefore should not be eligible to serve."

A woman on the committee leaned forward to her microphone. "Is he a member of the Republican Party?"

"I have to assume so," the chair said.

"Well, that's the only qualification he needs to meet," the woman said.

Jack had explained his position in great detail in his letter, but clearly no one had taken the time to read it. "If I may," he said. "The argument is that in order to be a fully recognized member of the party, one has to be eligible to vote. According to the Texas Election Code, Chapter Eleven, Section Two, to be a qualified voter an ex-convict must have completed their sentence as well as any period of probation ordered by the court. Mister Sempel has not yet completed his probation, and therefore is not a qualified voter in the state of Texas."

The committee members huddled together and discussed the matter for the better part of a minute. The chair made some notes, then adjusted his microphone.

"The Credentials Committee has reviewed your challenge to Waylon Sempel's selection as a delegate to the state convention, initiated in compliance with Rule 27 part B of the Republican Party of Texas Rules. Seeing as how Mister Sempel is currently on probation and therefore ineligible to participate in party activities, this challenge is upheld." With no discernible enthusiasm at all, he added, "Congratulations, Mister Patton—you're now a full-fledged state delegate."

18

U.S. ROUTE 90 hung low and drooping across the midsection of Texas like a belt struggling against a fat man's gut. Somewhere along the vast brown flatness between Sanderson ("the cactus capital of Texas!" according to sun-faded billboards) and the border town of Langtry, where Judge Roy Bean had once held court—literally—at the Jersey Lilly Saloon, a dark blue subcompact hatchback sat parked on the side of the highway. A magnet slapped onto the driver's-side door read "Rhinestone Maids" in frilly pink lettering. Inside, Fleming sat in silence with a middle-aged Hispanic woman. Both wore pink uniforms and aprons.

This was the Twenty-Third District, the largest in Texas by area, bordered on the west by the ever-thinning strand of the Rio Grande and, across it, Mexico. Spanish settlers had once labeled it "El Despoblado," meaning "the uninhabited," and little had changed in nearly two centuries. Where Fleming and the woman sat, cell phones were useless for twenty miles in either direction. They hadn't seen another car for ten minutes. The sun had just come up, and already the baked dry ground was shimmering with heat.

Fleming flipped idly through a dossier labeled "George Vestry." Sixty-eight years old. President of the local pistol club, and vice-president of the rifle club. Third-generation sheep rancher and owner of the Prickly Pear Inn in Sanderson. Weekly visitor to Del Rio via U.S. Route 90. Selected as a delegate for the state Republican convention, which he was scheduled to leave for later that day. Considered a shoo-in for a presidential elector slot by Langhorne and the rest of the team at the Nexus. Considered impervious to any available form of persuasion.

The satellite-based GPS tracker on Fleming's dash began to beep. She watched the screen as a dot appeared, then moved steadily across it each time the data refreshed.

She turned to the other woman. "*Es casi la hora,*" she said. *It's almost time.* On the horizon, glints of morning sunlight flashed from an oncoming car.

Fleming eased the hatchback onto the highway, accelerating slowly. It took a few minutes for the truck to catch up, and it was traveling so fast that it looked like it might pass her before she could make her move. As the truck glided over into the empty oncoming traffic lane to pass, Fleming drifted over as well. She slammed on the brakes and the truck rear-ended the hatchback hard. Fleming's passenger let out a scream of pain, or fear, or possibly both.

The momentum of the truck carried them several hundred feet down the highway before both vehicles came to a stop.

George Vestry stepped out of his truck, black felt Stetson not an inch out of place from the collision. "Just what in the hell you think you're doing?'" he called out.

Fleming's passenger got out, steadied herself, and approached Vestry. She began speaking quickly and in Spanish.

Vestry cupped his hands around his mouth and shouted, "You're in America! Speak English, you goddamn beaner!"

Fleming rolled down her window and called out to Vestry. "Excuse me... I think I'm hurt. I can't move my leg."

"Your own goddamn fault," Vestry muttered as he walked up to the driver side of the crushed hatchback. He leaned in through the window, the silver-tipped ends of his bolo tie dangling in front of Fleming's turned-away face. "What's wrong with your leg?" he said as he looked down at the floorboard. "It don't look crushed or anything."

Fleming turned her head back toward him, and for a moment he just stared, trying to figure out why she was wearing a gas mask. She grabbed his bolo and pulled him off balance into the cab; with her other hand she shoved the nozzle of a pressurized hose into his mouth and pulled the trigger.

Vestry gagged as yellowish-green gas came out the sides of his mouth. He tried to pull himself out of the car, but was crippled by involuntary retching and coughing. Fleming held fast to the bolo with one hand, and forced the nozzle deeper into Vestry's mouth.

His throat and lungs tried to reject the searing gas, and he launched spatters of blood across Fleming's face mask as he coughed. But after every cough he drew in more gas; soon blood was dripping from his nose and tears streamed from his bloodshot eyes. The coughing turned into a steady gurgle.

Fleming held fast to his bolo, focusing intently on the gold and silver Star of Texas emblem that adorned the slide lock. After a minute he had stopped struggling. After two minutes he had stopped breathing.

She was careful to move him back to his truck with a minimum of blood spillage. She positioned him in his seat and pulled the belt across his lap. Then she pulled out a thin strip of metal and wedged it into the belt lock as she fastened it. She gave it a few tests. The seat belt lock was jammed and would not release.

She walked back toward the hatchback, searching the ground for drops of blood. She found a couple near the shoulder, and covered them with dirt. As she double-checked the ground for evidence, she became aware of a faint sobbing. It was her passenger, sitting on the opposite side of the road, rocking back and forth as she wiped tears from her eyes.

"*Esta bien,*" Fleming said gently. "*Esta bien.*"

She wiped down the interior of the hatchback, then started it up and pulled a hundred feet down the highway. She braced her head back against the headrest, threw the car into reverse, and stomped on the gas pedal. She guided herself using the rear-view mirror, aiming straight for the front of Vestry's truck.

The impact shattered the hatchback's rear window and sent cleaning supplies flying onto the truck's hood. She dressed up the scene further, scattering sponges and mop heads across it. Then she smashed the truck's front window and tossed two bottles into the cab. One contained bleach, and the other ammonia; both were carefully scored along their fabrication seams, and split open upon impact. Fleming moved away quickly as the cab filled with smoky fumes.

She tossed the keys to the Hispanic woman. "Just stick to the story," Fleming said to her in Spanish. "Your husband already picked up the money in Acuña. They'll send you back to Mexico, and you and your family will live very well. If you change your story, you will stay here in prison. Understand?" The woman nodded nervously.

Fleming went back to the hatchback and removed all evidence of her presence: the GPS tracker; the file folder on George Vestry; and the green pressurized canister, complete with hose and nozzle, stamped with Chinese text and skull-and-crossbones symbols.

Less than a minute later, a black sedan approached and rolled to a stop, engine still running. The passenger door opened just a crack. "*Adios*," Fleming said to the other woman, then stepped into the sedan and disappeared.

The following morning, the *Del Rio News Herald* ran a story about a tragic traffic fatality that occurred on U.S. Route 90 over in Terrell County. The victim, George Vestry, was well-known and beloved in the tiny community of Sanderson. He had struck the rear of a hatchback driven by Marisol Gutierrez, an illegal immigrant who worked as a housekeeper in the area. Gutierrez had reportedly slammed on the brakes to avoid hitting an armadillo as it crossed the highway.

The impact sent bottles of cleaning chemicals, which had been stored in the trunk of the hatchback, into the cab of Vestry's truck. There, they ruptured and combined to create a cloud of toxic chlorine gas. Vestry was apparently unable to escape the toxic gas cloud due to a jammed seat belt lock, and died from respiratory failure. By all appearances, it was the very definition of a freak accident.

According to the article, Gutierrez was taken into custody by U.S. Immigration and Customs Enforcement, and awaited deportation back to Mexico.

19

THE NEXT MORNING at the convention center, all the temporary setups and stopgap preps were gone: the apparatus of the convention was fully assembled and chugging away. In the main foyer, thousands of people formed snake-like queues that appeared to have neither head nor tail. For all Jack knew, they could have all been segments of the same massive line, coiling through the entire convention center and terminating in a single card table with a folded sign that read "Registration."

Jack soon discovered that everything was broken down by district. This gave him a brief panic when he remembered that his district had only recently changed, and he could not remember the number of the new one. After checking through his paperwork, he approached the registration desk and answered confidently, "Congressional District Twenty-Five."

The no-nonsense woman behind the desk smiled tersely. "I

need your Senatorial District," she said.

"I thought both Senators served the whole state."

"I mean your state Senatorial District," she said. "For the state Senate."

"They're not the same?"

The woman shook her head.

Jack couldn't help but laugh. "Just when I think I've got all this finally figured out, I realize that I don't know a damn thing."

The woman gave him a sympathetic nod. "Why don't you show me on this map?" she said. Once she helped him find the answer, he wrote in large block letters across the top of his program: "SD-24."

Next to the registration area was an expansive exhibit hall filled with a boggling array of vendors and other exhibitors. Jack checked his watch and, realizing he had some time to kill before the opening speeches, passed through the hall.

Most of the exhibitors were either state-level candidates, regional organizations like the Texas State Rifle Association, or lobbying groups. But it was the odd, occasional entrepreneurs that caught Jack's interest. One booth, sponsored by a major sausage link producer, devoted itself to celebrating the joys of breakfast. Another offered fine art prints that featured Jesus, bathed in crepuscular rays of heavenly light, inspiring the Founding Fathers as they wrote the Constitution.

For pure commercial crassness, though, Jack's favorite was a booth where convention-goers could get a custom-made sports magazine cover featuring themselves delivering a knockout blow to the current president. Jack struck up a conversation with the guy running the booth in between a steady stream of customers.

"So if you don't mind me asking," Jack said, "do you have to pay for this booth space?"

The guy nodded. "Thousand bucks. But I'll clear that before the day's over, and the rest is gonna be gravy."

"Wow. So do you do this all the time? Like, state fairs and stuff?"

"Yep. Just switch out the background image and you can do this anywhere, anytime. But this spring's been crazy with the GOP conventions."

"Oh yeah?"

"Did Louisiana last week, and Georgia a few weeks ago. Before that was Oklahoma, and Utah and Colorado back-to-back in April. Utah, man, I had a line all the way down the aisle. Next week is Virginia, then probably Idaho, and hopefully we'll be at the national convention in Tampa in August. That's where the *real* money is."

As the start time drew near, Jack headed over to the massive arena adjacent to the main convention building. The floor and loge were broken into sections, each marked by tall signs indicating which district the delegates in that section represented. Jack found the sign marked "24," and his heart sank: there were several hundred delegates and alternates just within his district. He had always known the odds were against him being chosen as an elector, but it was easy to ignore odds when they existed only in the abstract; the crowd in the District 24 section was a concrete depiction of dismal probability that, once he had seen it, could not be dismissed.

Still, Jack made an effort to talk to the delegates around him, explaining his situation and his desire to become an elector. At the same time, he made sure to ask others about their goals. Many hoped to be chosen as national delegates, responsible for selecting the Republican presidential candidate at the national convention. A few hoped to be chosen as members of the Republican National Committee, which sounded quite important even though Jack had no idea what it actually did. No one else he talked with expressed a desire to become an elector; he took that as a positive sign.

Jack's attempts at self-promotion were interrupted by a blaring fanfare, during which the governor took the stage. His opening remarks drew polite if not entirely enthusiastic applause, focusing on how he had grown the Texas economy and fought back the power-hungry vipers of the federal government along the way. The speech was interrupted by occasional boos from different groups in the crowd, which surprised Jack.

The governor was followed by several state officials that Jack was ashamed to say he could not identify by name, like the Comptroller and State Attorney General. The Attorney General drew some rousing applause when he railed against voter fraud, but after several speeches the crowd was growing restless.

Finally the State Party Chair took to the podium and called the convention to order.

The convention broke into Senatorial District Caucuses in smaller conference rooms. There weren't enough chairs, so Jack and about fifty others were left standing along the margins of the room. The temporary District Caucus Chair conducted a roll call, which seemed endless. Once all the district delegates were accounted for, they went about Party business.

Jack tried to follow along, but between the ambient noise in the large room and the fast pace at which business was conducted, he got lost somewhere in the middle of the various committee appointments and votes. All Jack knew for certain was that he voted for a whole lot of temporary something-or-others to become permanent something-or-others.

During a lull in the voting, Jack turned to the man standing next to him. "Do you know when we vote on national delegates and electors?" he asked.

"Not till tomorrow or the day after, I don't think," the man said. "That's at the Congressional District Caucus."

Jack felt his body fold inward at the news. He thought he just might collapse to the floor and ask someone to kick him when it was time to vote on the interesting stuff.

When the day was done and Jack got back to his hotel room, there was a message waiting for him. "This is Bruce Wells from the *Fort Worth Star-Telegram*. If possible, I'd like to speak with you for a story I'm writing about the convention. Please call me back any time tonight."

Jack called him back, and the reporter picked up on the first ring. "Got dinner plans?" Wells asked. "There's a great steak house a couple blocks from you."

When Jack arrived, Wells was standing out by the curb, finishing a cigarette. The exterior of the building had the understated elegance of a very old structure that had been lovingly restored. "Did this used to be a theater or something?" Jack asked.

"Bathhouse, actually," Wells said. "Back before the houses here had indoor plumbing. The place is supposed to be haunted. Came here to write a story about the haunting a few years ago, and I've been coming back ever since."

Inside, the restaurant was impeccably appointed with gleaming brass and rippling walnut. The entire center of the second floor was open, giving the upper floor the appearance of a ringed balcony.

After the greeter seated them, Wells pulled out his smartphone and set it to record. "Do you mind?" he asked, gesturing to the phone.

Jack shook his head.

"So I've heard just a little about your story," Wells said, "your father and all that. Would you mind telling me in your own words?"

Jack took a deep breath and launched into his tale. He had told it enough now that it had developed into a sort of performance; he knew which parts to draw out for maximum drama, and which parts to gloss over for the sake of pace and rhythm.

Every so often, Wells prodded him for some additional information. By the time Jack finished, their bone-in ribeyes were being delivered. Wells said, "Fantastic story. I think it'll be perfect for the Sunday edition."

"Wow. Really?" Jack was taken aback at the notion that someone would find any aspect of his life interesting enough to read about. Before he could catch himself, he thought, *Boy, Dad would get a kick out of this.*

"I think I've got everything I need as far as copy," Wells said. "But we'll need a photographer to snap some art."

"Art?"

"We'll need a picture of you to go with the story. How about tomorrow afternoon after the convention lets out? The

Water Gardens would make a good shot. And you have the pen with you, right? The one your dad left you?"

"Yeah. It's in my suitcase."

"Perfect. Bring it. I'll have somebody call you to set up a time."

With work out of the way, Wells dug into his steak and the conversation became more relaxed. "So you're from down around Nobles?" he said. "My sister used to live there."

"Oh yeah?"

"She's actually the one that tipped me to your story, even though she doesn't live there anymore. Maggie Wells. Ever heard of her?"

Jack shook his head.

"Well, actually it's Maggie Landreau now. I keep forgetting. She divorced the guy after two years, but kept his name. Can't say I understand that."

Jack smiled to himself. Everything suddenly made sense. "Maggie Landreau?"

"You do know her, then."

"Can't say we've met," Jack said. "But I hear she makes one hell of a bowl of red."

20

On the second day of the convention, Jack brought his father's pen with him—partly so he could head straight to the meeting with the *Star-Telegram* photographer when the day's business was done, and partly in an attempt to impress his fellow district delegates. He knew the pen held a certain power over other Party members he had shown it to, largely because of its association with President Reagan. In primitive tribes, anthropologists would have called it contagious magic; here, they called it heritage.

After another full day of committee meetings, tedious debates of process and wording, and votes on party positions that he never knew existed, Jack was eager to get out of the convention center. He was waiting at the Water Gardens when the *Star-Telegram* photographer arrived. Bruce had said to meet the guy at "the part that looks like Picasso built a staircase and then left the bathtub running upstairs." Jack had no idea what that meant when he heard it, but then he saw it for himself, and couldn't think of a better way to describe it. Water cascaded down giant, angular concrete terraces to a churning pool at the bottom. Standing on the path that twisted down through it, the whole thing gave him the impression of a surreal, flooded amphitheater.

The photographer took some pictures of Jack standing near the bottom of the pool, holding his father's increasingly famous pen. The photographer scrolled through the shots on his digital camera, said "good luck" to Jack, and was gone. The whole thing took less than five minutes. Jack spent the rest of the evening sitting in his hotel room alone, eating a take-out sandwich and watching old sitcom reruns.

On the third day, they finally settled into the second Congressional district caucus meeting—the one where national delegates and electors were chosen. Jack began working the crowd, pressing palms and turning every conversation around to his own story. He wasn't accustomed to being so forward with his wants; even as a business owner dependent upon a steady stream of new clients, he had never really needed to aggressively pursue new projects. He built up his client base through solid work and positive word of mouth.

But this was different. He wasn't pursuing a spot as a presidential elector for himself... not really. It was all for his father. That fundamental difference gave him license to control the conversation, play upon emotions and sympathies, ask for support. It gave him permission to be a politician.

He even pledged his support to several people who were seeking delegate slots for the national convention, in exchange for their consideration. In fact, he lost track of how many delegates he said he'd vote for. Definitely more than enough to fill the three available slots and three alternate slots.

When the chair called for nominations for national delegates, dozens of people shouted out. The chair methodically wrote down every candidate's name, then allowed each one to make a one-minute speech. More than half the candidates were clearly from the Bennett camp, much like the ones who had overrun the courthouse at the Nobles County convention. After the fourth or fifth Bennett supporter began speaking, a middle-aged man near Jack shouted out, "Randell already won the Texas primary. We need Randell delegates, not Bennett fanatics!" About half the crowd cheered the man, but a small percentage booed and shouted even louder above the cheers.

Even once the speeches were done, the voting process was tedious. Instead of just giving the slots to the candidates that received the highest number of votes, everyone had to vote on one candidate for the first delegate slot. If no candidate received a majority of the vote, then the two candidates who got the fewest votes were eliminated, and everyone voted again.

The Bennett supporters quickly realized that they had to throw their support behind a single candidate to avoid being knocked out of the running. Still, the pro-Bennett candidates failed to make it past the first few rounds. In all, it took eleven votes just to pick the first delegate. Then the whole process—including the call for nominations—began all over again. And then once more for the final delegate slot. And then *three more times* for the alternate slots. A Bennett supporter finally made it into one of the alternate slots, probably because everyone just wanted to be done with it.

Finally, once the national delegates were set, the chair called for nominations for presidential electors. Jack opened his mouth to call out his own name, but was beaten to the punch by someone across the room shouting, "I nominate Floyd Hubert!" This was followed by a quick "Second!"

Jack had no idea who Floyd Hubert was, but he was quick to jump in and nominate himself immediately after. Some kind anonymous soul seconded the nomination, and he was on the candidate list.

He ran his speech over in his head, nervous about the short time limit. Could he hit all the major points without sounding glib about his father's death? The chair called for Floyd to speak first, and the crowd grew hushed as an elderly man in an old but perfectly preserved Army uniform was wheeled to the center of the congregation.

With some help, Floyd stood and smoothed his uniform with his shaky, weathered hands. With his bald head and sagging face, he reminded Jack of a turkey, but he commanded the attention and respect of the crowd like a five-star general. His voice was hoarse, but it carried in the silent room.

"The first time I was eligible to vote," Floyd said, "was in Nineteen and Fifty-Two. I was in Korea with the Twenty-Fourth Infantry. We were out west of the Hwachon Dam pushing back the Chinese, and we took mortar fire." He rapped a knuckle against his right thigh, and to Jack's surprise, the sound rang out clear.

"They got most of my leg, and I ended up back at a MASH unit for, oh, I think a month. They had me on some heavy medication for a couple weeks, and when I finally came out of it, they told me Eisenhower won the election. So there I was, fightin' Commies overseas, and I never even had a chance to vote." The crowd let out a sympathetic "Aww," but Floyd just gave a raspy laugh.

"Anyhow, I've never missed an election since then, and I've always voted Republican. I think I'd like to be an elector before I die, just to make up for that vote I missed back in Fifty-Two. Thank you." Floyd nodded, then sank back into his wheelchair.

The crowd erupted into wild applause. Inside, Jack just withered. There was no possible way he could compete with that. He didn't even *want* to compete with that. He suddenly wished he could withdraw his name from contention. What was the point? Even if he somehow won, he would look like the jerk who stole the spot from a genuine war hero.

Once the crowd settled, the chair called for Jack's speech. He halfheartedly stumbled through his story, painfully aware of how trivial it sounded in the wake of Floyd's tale. Still, the crowd offered polite applause afterward and several people patted his shoulder in support.

"Okay then, let's vote," said the Chair. "First, everyone in favor of Floyd Hubert, raise a hand." Jack was afraid to look out across what he knew was a forest of extended arms, so he kept his head down and occupied himself by flipping through his convention program.

After an agonizing few minutes of tallying, the chair said, "Mister Hubert carries a majority, no need to proceed. Congratulations Mister Hubert." The crowd applauded once again, and that was that. They never even called for a vote on Jack's nomination. His dream of becoming an elector was done.

*　　　　　　*　　　　　　*

When he got back to his room, Jack figured that he owed Bruce Wells a call. The reporter seemed energized about the story and the art. "Everything looks great," he said.

"Listen," Jack said, "before you get too excited about this... I didn't get picked."

"Really? Man, I thought they'd eat that story up."

"Yeah, well, they were already stuffed by the time they got to me."

After a brief pause, Wells said, "Sorry to hear that, but no worries. The story's still a go. In fact, it might even be more poignant now."

The next day, Jack beat the rush out of town. On his way home, he called Vera Lynn and broke the bad news. "You did everything you could," she said.

"So did you," he said. "I got interviewed by somebody at the *Star-Telegram*."

"Is that right?" she asked.

"Comes out in today's paper, so too late to matter, I guess. But still, it was a hell of a try. Thanks."

"For what?"

"The guy that interviewed me. Maggie Landreau's brother. I don't suppose you happened to call Maggie and see if she could pull some strings?"

"I have no idea what you're talkin' about," she said, but even over the phone Jack could tell that she was smiling.

When he got back to Nobles, Jack bought a copy of the *Star-Telegram* and drove out to Marbletop Hill. It was the first time he had been to the cemetery since the funeral. The headstone was in place, and the grass on his father's grave looked as lush and undisturbed as the plots that surrounded it. It was still before noon, but the sun was already beating down mercilessly. Jack sat on the edge of the headstone, opened the newspaper, and read the article aloud to his father.

When he finished, he said, "I know you always hated those liberal big-city rags. But Dad, you gotta admit, that was a pretty good story." He folded the paper and tucked it under his arm. "I just wish it would've had a different ending."

He sat in silence on his father's headstone, listening to the chatter of bugs and the occasional murmur of a passing car. And for the first time since his father died, Jack buried his face in his hands and cried.

21

"THE LIST IS IN," Langhorne said, and handed the sheet to Candace. She began copying names to an empty whiteboard.

"Thirty-eight electors total... one from each Congressional district, and two at-large electors for the Senatorial districts. If all the swing states fall to Randell, then we need twenty of those thirty-eight electors. Thanks to our chaff deployment strategy, we ended up with four ringers and two Sleeping Dogs in position, so that leaves fourteen more. This is where the hard work begins."

"My guy Robeson is in," Miles said after scanning the list, and pumped his fist until he noticed that everyone else was staring at him.

As Candace got farther down the list, she said, "One of our shoo-ins didn't make it. George Vestry. Wonder what happened."

"Who cares," said Langhorne. "At least he's not our problem. Back to the list. Grant, you'll be in charge of the field researchers gathering intel on the electors. Miles, you'll assist with compiling and evaluating the data."

"So what are we looking for, exactly?" Miles asked.

"Everything," Langhorne said. "You have resources at your disposal that most governments would kill for. Use them. We need to know more about these people than their best friends and their spouses put together. If one of our targets has a bowel movement in the morning, I expect you to know whether or not it had corn in it."

"We should start by grouping the targets by tier," Candace said. "Tier Zero is any target we've already locked down as a sure vote. Tier One targets would be the electors most likely to flip, but that haven't flipped yet. Tier Two would be ones where we have less leverage. Tier Three would be unlikely to flip, and Tier Four would be our write-off, no-chance-in-hell electors. So we start with Tier One and see what we can get, then keep moving down until we hit fourteen that we can convert up to Tier Zero."

They went through the list, doing preliminary research to rank the unknowns. Six of the electors were marked with "Tier Zero." Robeson and five others were marked "Tier One."

Floyd Hubert, decorated Korean War veteran, was placed on Tier Four.

22

The house was a ranch-style brick built in the 1950s on a road outside of Gurston, about twenty miles north of Nobles. It had once been someone's idea of the perfect suburban plan: a few miles outside the city so a homeowner could have a spacious lot, but close enough to quickly get to anywhere a person might need. Instead of flourishing over the years, however, it had simply died off. As homeowners got older, the appeal of living farther away from doctors and the post office and the grocery store seemed to fade, as did the ability to care for a spacious plot of land.

Several of the houses along the road were clearly not lived in, with weeds and weather slowly reclaiming the structures. Others were rented out to families that, for one reason or another, organized society had spat outside the city limits. Rusting car bodies and damaged children's toys were scattered across the yards.

But there was one house on the road that still retained the bright, clean appearance of a bygone era. Fleming checked the address on the mailbox, then pulled into the driveway.

It took nearly a minute for the person inside to answer the doorbell. Every ten seconds or so, a muffled "Hold your horses" or "I'm comin'" could be heard from the front room. When the door finally opened, Fleming smiled brightly and held out her hand. "Mister Hubert? Samantha Creed, *Lone Star Soldier* magazine. Pleasure to meet you."

Floyd Hubert looked quite different from his appearance at the Republican state convention. He wore a striped Western shirt with snap pockets and loose-fitting blue jeans. His bald, freckled head was capped with a spotless shantung straw cowboy hat. And most notably, although his journey to the door had taken some time, there was not a wheelchair in sight.

"Yep," Floyd said, and took her hand briefly before turning away and shuffling toward the couch in his stocking feet. "Come on in then. Have a seat."

"You have a lovely home," Fleming said. "Do you live here on your own?"

"Yep. My son stops by every Sunday, puts a mirror in front of my face to make sure I'm still kickin'." He let out a laugh that could have easily been mistaken for a wheezing cough.

"So you don't rely on regular homecare?"

"Why? Do I look that bad?"

Fleming laughed. "Not at all."

"You seem awful concerned about my health. I thought this was gonna be about my service."

"Absolutely," Fleming said. She pulled out her smartphone and began tapping on its keypad. "Do you mind if I take notes as we go?"

"Might not do much good. My stories change every time I tell 'em." Again he let out a wheezy laugh.

"I've heard your story, Mister Hubert, and there's certainly no need to embellish it. It's amazing. The reason I'm asking these health-related questions is because our readership skews senior. I think they'll be especially interested in hearing about how able-bodied you are, considering the fact that you're a combat-injured veteran."

"I get by," Floyd said.

"So you don't rely on anyone to take you into town, to the store or anything like that."

Floyd shook his head. "They ain't taken my license away yet, so I'll keep on driving till they do."

"That's fantastic that you're still so independent. My understanding is that you had a double bypass a few years ago."

"Yep." He tapped a finger to his chest. "Got a pacemaker put in too, keeps me on track."

Fleming smiled and tapped away on her phone. "Isn't technology amazing?"

"Sure enough. Say, can I get you a drink? Water? Soda pop? I should've asked when you came in, but I haven't had a guest in a while, so I apologize." Floyd stood creakily and shuffled toward the kitchen.

"Water would be great, thanks," she said, and continued punching keys on her phone. "You know, the really amazing part of technology nowadays is how much stuff you can do with the smallest devices."

Floyd grunted agreement as he leaned into the refrigerator.

"This smartphone, for example. We call it a phone, but it

really does so much more. I can listen to music, check my email... I can even do this." Fleming tapped the screen and Floyd's hunched frame jolted upright. After a second he unfroze, dropping the drinks from his hands and staggering backward into the dining room table. He clutched at his chest with a trembling hand.

"You know what else is amazing?" Fleming said. "Companies spend billions of dollars coming up with fancy encryption and security systems to protect all kinds of machines from being hacked. Computers, ATMs, phones, all that stuff. But your average electronic medical implant? No security whatsoever." She tapped her screen again, and again Floyd went rigid. Afterward, he fell to the floor and let out an unintelligible moan.

"Did you know that if you time it right, you can use a pacemaker to cause cardiac arrest? You have to disrupt the normal beat at just the right point. Sometimes it takes a few jolts, and I'm out of practice, so bear with me." She zapped him again, and his hand—which had stiffened into a rigid claw—finally fell limp.

"Winner winner, chicken dinner," she said. Floyd's chest stopped moving, and he let out one last leaky gasp.

"It's too bad your son isn't coming till Sunday," she said. "I don't think he's going to need a mirror this time. I imagine that by then the smell will be a dead giveaway."

Fleming strolled over to the refrigerator and picked up the water bottle Floyd had dropped. "Thanks for the drink," she said, and twisted off the cap as she headed out into the scorching summer sun, locking the door behind her.

23

"Good news for us," Langhorne said. "Floyd Hubert died." He walked over to one of the white boards and found Hubert's name, under the column labeled "Tier Four," and wiped it clean.

"Hubert," Platt repeated. "Which one was that?"

"Korean War vet," Candace said. "Purple Heart. How did he die?"

"Strangely enough, he died of a purple heart. Or idiopathic dilated cardiomyopathy, to quote the death certificate."

"So who's replacing him?" Miles asked.

"You'll know when I know."

"Whoever it is," Platt said, "we're bound to have a better chance of flipping them. That guy was beyond persuasion."

"Where are we with the Tier One targets?" Langhorne asked. Grant walked over to the board labeled "Tier One" and pointed to each of the eight names on the list as he rattled off their weaknesses. "Adulterer, open to bribery, owes money on a failing business, adulterer, adulterer, keeps a secret profile on a gay matchmaking service, addicted to Vicodin, and adulterer."

"So if we turn all eight," Platt said, "that gives us twelve total."

"So we still need eight more on top of those."

"Which ones didn't vote for Randell in the primary?" Candace asked.

Grant pulled up a spreadsheet on his tablet, and as he went through it, he put check marks next to ten names on the board. "Those are the ones that didn't vote Randell."

"Does that matter though?" asked Miles. "I mean, once they pick their guy, Republicans sure as hell know how to toe the party line."

"It could help when we get to our late-game strategy," Langhorne said, pointing to a whiteboard that had the word "Scandal" written on it in large letters.

"Now... where are we with Robeson?" he asked Miles.

"The guy's like a money pit," Miles said. "He called and asked for another half million."

Langhorne thought it over. "Fine. But after that, he's been paid in full. Time to cash in our chips." Langhorne rapped his stack of papers on the edge of the desk. "That's all for now... back to work."

Candace followed Langhorne into his office and shut the door behind her. "Tell me it wasn't us," she said.

"What?"

"Hubert," she answered. "Tell me we didn't do that."

Langhorne laid his hands gently on her shoulders. "The

man was eighty-two. A stiff wind could've done him in."

"And yet the death certificate doesn't say anything about a stiff wind." She lowered her voice despite the closed door. "We both know there are at least a dozen ways to make a death look enough like a heart attack to escape attention. Just say it wasn't us."

Langhorne pulled back. "You know, things may get messy before we're done here. That won't be an issue for you... will it?"

"I'm fine with pushing the boundaries to see this thing through," she said. "I just need to know that the boundaries still exist."

Langhorne stared into her eyes, cool, unblinking. "It wasn't us," he said. "But in the future, if you're not truly prepared to hear the answer—whatever it may be—then don't ask the question."

24

"Jack Patton?" the voice on the other end of the phone asked.

"It is. Who's this?"

"Please hold for Eleanor Craddock." Jack couldn't place the name, but for some reason, he felt like he should know it.

"Jack, Eleanor Craddock here. How are you?"

"Fine," he said. "And you?"

"You may not remember me, but I'm the Chair of the Republican Party of Texas. Sorry I didn't get a chance to meet you at the convention."

Suddenly Jack got a hazy image of a woman at the podium on the first day of the convention. There were so many speeches, and it had seemed so long ago. "It's a pleasure," he said. "Is there something I can do for you?"

"Well, I'm hoping I can do something for you. Somebody handed me a copy of that article the *Star-Telegram* did on you, and it really moved me. I didn't know your father, but I know a couple of people who did, and they would've went on all day about him if I didn't stop them."

"I appreciate that."

"As you know, presidential elector slots are pretty damn hard to come by. But sometimes, due to unforeseen circumstances, we end up with a vacancy. Turns out your district now has an opening."

"Did something happen to Floyd?" he asked, genuine concern briefly driving out any excitement.

"Mister Hubert has unfortunately passed away," she said.

Jack had a hard time wrapping his head around the idea. Floyd must have been over eighty, and Jack only met him once, but even in a wheelchair he seemed like an active participant in the world. Much more so than his own father was at the end. "I'm... really sorry to hear that," he said. "Do they know the cause?"

"Looks like it was just one of those things. He'd had a bypass before, and a pacemaker, so his heart wasn't in the best shape. But let's not dwell on that. The good news is that we'd like you to be an elector. We just have some paperwork we need you to fill out to make it official."

"I can come right now," Jack said. "Just tell me where."

*　　　　　*　　　　　*

The Republican Party of Texas headquarters were just a couple of miles from Jack's office, a block west of the Capitol. The building was nondescript and strangely unmarked regarding its tenants; the only visible signage, placed in most of the ground-floor windows, read "Space for Lease." Jack went up to the second floor as instructed, and found an elegant, quiet reception area decorated with old maps of the Republic of Texas. It could have easily been mistaken for a dentist's office. After the receptionist confirmed his appointment, he was escorted through a security door to an expansive, bustling office.

Eleanor Craddock welcomed him warmly. She wore a black and white houndstooth blazer with such a large pattern that it looked like she had been engulfed in a swarm of horseflies. Her dark brown hair was perfectly styled, like a frozen wave. As she talked, his eyes were irresistibly drawn to her shiny chin.

"Jack, we appreciate you stepping up in such a timely manner," she said. "We've just got some paperwork that needs to be filled out before you can officially be considered for an elector spot." She motioned to a chair inside her office, and he sat.

"So tell me," she said, settling in behind her desk, "who's been your pick for candidate?"

"Randell," he said. "I know the convention is still a ways out, but he seems like the obvious choice."

"What if the party chose a different candidate?" she asked. "Say, someone more focused on preserving American values instead of someone focused on fixing the economy?"

Jack had never really considered the possibility. There were certainly some candidates that he considered a bit extreme for his tastes, but he never really envisioned them securing the nomination. However, he sensed that Eleanor's question was more about sussing out loyalty than weighing the merits of potential presidential candidates. "I'd vote for whoever got the nomination, if that's what you're asking."

"Good," she said. "Dedication to the party is a big thing for us when we're choosing electors. No offense to you, but electors usually come from a very trusted group of people who've been active in the party for a long time. Former governors, state senators, mayors, those sorts of folks. We know your father was like that, and we're glad to see you follow in his footsteps."

She slid a sheet of paper across the desk to Jack. At the top was the Republican Party of Texas seal. "If you could, just read out that text in the middle and then sign it."

Jack cleared his throat. "I, John Arthur Patton, a registered Republican voter in the state of Texas, do hereby pledge, in accordance with the rules and requirements of the Republican Party of Texas, to cast my vote in the Electoral College for the Republican nominees for President and Vice President as determined by the national party delegates and Republican National Committee."

"All right then," Eleanor said, "just sign the bottom and you are good to go." He signed and handed it back to her.

"Just one more thing I have to mention," she said. "When voters in your district cast their ballot on election day, they're not voting for president or vice president. They're voting for *you*. I don't mean that as a figure of speech. They are literally voting for you to go cast a vote on their behalf at the electoral college. I cannot overstate the importance of your role in choosing our next president.

"Because of that, it's crucial that you conduct yourself in a manner that reflects well on the party and the candidates. We prefer electors to avoid the limelight, stay away from controversial events or demonstrations, and always, *always* support the party platform. If we hear of anything that gives us pause... well, let's just say that electors don't have to die to be replaced."

"Understood," Jack said.

"We'll have some specifics about signing the elector ballot to go over, but not until after November, which is when you'd officially be appointed as an elector. And you can always give a shout if you have any questions. But other than that..." She stood and offered her hand. "Let's get out there and win an election."

Jack left the party headquarters feeling as if he were hovering six inches above the ground. He had tried so hard to earn a spot as an elector, and failed despite his best efforts. And then suddenly it was just handed to him. Whether it was karma or happenstance, he wasn't about to argue. He was just grateful that he would be able to fulfill his promise to his father after all.

Jack drove back to his office, oblivious to the black sedan that followed him at a distance.

25

"John Arthur Patton," Grant read from a file folder. "Goes by Jack. Forty years old, divorced, no children, no pets. Has a condo near Zilker Park, but he's still registered to vote out in Nobles, which is why he's an elector for the Twenty-Fifth District. Owns a graphic design business called Roundabout Design on South Congress that does okay, not great, but doesn't have any outstanding debt."

"Has this guy got *any* pressure points we can exploit?" Platt asked.

"Does he date?" Fleming offered.

"Not that we can find."

"Anything else?" asked Miles.

"He does have a sister who lives in Nobles."

"Older or younger?"

"Older."

"Hm. Are they close?"

"Doesn't look like it, but according to his phone records, he's been talking to her more over the past six months. It started after his father passed away. Speaking of which," Grant tossed a section of newspaper onto the table. It was the Sunday Feature section of the *Fort Worth Press-Telegram*; the cover showed Jack Patton holding a pen. "His father is the reason he became an elector."

"How important is this guy?" asked Fleming.

"If everything else pans out perfectly," Grant said, "we've got nineteen electors so far. That means he'd be the winning vote."

"I'll take this one," Fleming said. "I'll become his girlfriend, then you guys can kidnap me and hold me hostage until the vote."

"You wanna date this guy?" asked Platt, slightly wounded.

"Grow up," she said. "It's a job. If you don't have leverage, you make your own leverage."

"You guys are looking at this all wrong," Candace said. "Jack Patton is our new best friend. Honey versus vinegar. The guy's a moderate conservative at best, and not at all interested in politics. Give him the right reason and he'll flip on his own."

"The right reason being what?" asked Miles.

"That's what we have to find out," she said.

"So maybe we should be looking into the dad, you think?" asked Grant.

"It always comes down to incentives," Langhorne said. "It sounds like we'll have to create one. Fleming, do your thing. Everyone else, back to work."

When everyone had dispersed to their own desks, Candace did a web search for George Vestry, the shoo-in elector who somehow failed to show up on their final list. She found the article about his death in the *Del Rio News Herald*. She made a few notes on a small notepad, then closed the browser window, slipped the pad into her desk, and locked the drawer.

26

"CONGRATULATIONS for officially being part of the problem," Silas said to Jack, raising his bottle of Shiner Bock in mock salute. They were at Güero's, a funky and perennially crowded taco bar just a few blocks from the office on South Congress.

"Thanks?" Jack said.

"No disrespect," said Silas. "Noble cause, honor your father, blah blah blah. But the electoral college is a broken-ass relic that ought to be taken out in a field and shot square in the head like a rabid animal."

"So the Founding Fathers got it all wrong, huh?"

"In this case, they sure did. Did you know that the president was originally supposed to be chosen by Congress? The electoral college was a half-assed compromise for the framers who thought Congress shouldn't be allowed to choose the president directly. And here's why it was half-assed: most of them thought that aside from George Washington, no candidate was likely to ever get a majority of the electoral votes—which meant that Congress would get to decide the winner anyway."

"It's a good thing we've got you to tell us what the framers of the Constitution were thinking when they wrote it."

"Don't take my word for it," Silas said. "They told us themselves. Seriously, this isn't wild speculation. Look at their own words."

"Yeah, well, say what you want, but in the end they decided to let the people choose their own leader."

"No," said Silas. "They didn't. They decided to let a handful of electors choose their leader."

"You're just playing with semantics. People choose the electors."

"Not back then. Most states had their legislatures choose the electors. So even ignoring the fact that only ten to fifteen percent of the population was even allowed to vote at all, those voters *still* had no say in choosing their president. That was true for the first four elections in our country's history. The Founding Fathers did such a great job coming up with our election system that they had to completely scrap it and do the whole thing over fifteen years later. That's how we got the Twelfth Amendment."

"Whatever, but now, people choose their electors. It's a pretty direct process."

"And yet, no state is required to allow voters to choose their electors. If they wanted, they could have the state legislature do it, just like in the old days. They could have three old men go into a closet and spin a bottle if they wanted."

"But no state would do that, so it's a moot point. Just admit it: even with the electoral college, voters basically get to choose their president."

"Sure. Basically. But what about when voters choose one president while the electoral college chooses a different one?"

"Is this going to be more whining about the popular vote? You have to win the electoral college. That's how it works. And it's worked pretty damn good for a couple centuries."

"Pretty damn good? Really? Out of fifty-six presidential elections in our nation's history, we've had four occasions where the person that became president was *not* the person that got the most votes from eligible American voters. So if you want to believe that the point of our government is to enact the will of the people, that's a seven percent failure rate. Can you imagine if a car maker had the same failure rate? So one out of every fourteen cars the company made just randomly exploded while driving down the road? How long do you think that company would stay in business?"

"You know it's not the same thing," Jack said.

"You're right. In one case, you might kill a few passengers. In the other, you might wreck an entire country. The United States has inspired the creation of democracies all around the world for almost two hundred and fifty years. Do you know how many of those democracies also adopted our electoral college system?" He pinched his index finger and thumb together to form a giant zero.

Jack swigged his beer. "This is what I get for making friends with a Poli Sci major in college," he said. "It's all coming back to haunt me."

"In all seriousness, though," Silas said, "I know I'm coming off like a bit of a dick-"

"A bit?"

"-but I'm sure your dad would be proud. So for real... congrats."

"So since you know everything about elections," Jack said, "let me ask you: how exactly does somebody win the popular vote but not the electoral vote? I never got how that worked. I mean, the electoral votes reflect the popular vote. If you get the most popular votes, why wouldn't you get the most electoral votes too?"

"It's because of the way electoral votes are distributed. Most states are winner-take-all, meaning whoever wins the state gets all the electoral votes."

"Yeah..."

"So whoever gets the most votes in a state gets everything, even if that person just barely wins. Now suppose you've got two candidates." Silas pulled out a pen and began scribbling on a napkin. He drew two columns, one labeled "Candidate A" and one labeled "Candidate B."

"They're both trying to win in a hypothetical country," he continued. "Let's call it Jacksylvania. Jacksylvania has three states. Each state has three residents, and is worth one electoral vote. In the northern state, two people vote for Candidate A, and one votes for Candidate B." Silas drew two hash marks under the Candidate A column, and a single one under Candidate B.

"But in the central state, all three vote for Candidate B." He drew three more lines in the "B" column.

"In the southern state, the vote breaks down same as the northern state—two votes for Candidate A, and one for Candidate B." Silas added the lines in their respective columns.

"So? Who wins?"

Jack looked at the columns. "Candidate A only got four votes, and Candidate B got five votes."

"But Candidate A won two electoral votes, and Candidate B only got one electoral vote. So Candidate A wins even though he gets less popular votes than the other guy."

Jack stared at the napkin. "Huh. How about that."

"So it's all about how you divvy things up. Pretty much the same thing happens at the state level too. Politicians on both sides end up redrawing their state's Congressional districts to try and keep their side in control of as much of the state as possible. And you end up with ridiculous-looking districts that look like squiggly monsters. But you want to hear the worst part?" Silas asked.

"Because that's not enough?"

"Imagine that the central state of Jacksylvania has ten people instead of three people, but still only gets one electoral vote. It's possible that Candidate B could get a three-fourths majority of the popular vote and still lose."

"No, I know for a fact that that's wrong," Jack said. "The number of electors is determined by population. So if the central state has a higher population, it should have more electors."

"It should," Silas said. "But that's not the way it works in the real world, because it isn't proportional on the low end. Check this out: the state of Wyoming gets one electoral vote for roughly every 190,000 people. The state of Texas gets one electoral vote for every 675,000 people. So the vote of a Wyoming citizen is three and a half times more important than the vote of a Texas citizen. Not exactly equal representation."

"But that's because if it didn't have more electoral power, Wyoming would get steamrolled in Congress."

"Why shouldn't it? It has less people. It shouldn't have a disproportionately loud voice."

"Because we're the United *States*. All the states should get a say."

"I guess it all comes down to how you look at things," Silas said. "Are we a first and foremost a country, or are we a collection of states?"

"You say that," said Jack, "as you're sitting in a state that used to be its own country."

"God bless the Republic of Texas," Silas said loudly, and held up his beer. Half a dozen other diners joined in his salute.

27

The black sedan nosed into the empty parking space in front of Roundabout Design, steam pouring out from under its hood.

"That's trouble for somebody," Marlene said, peering over her monitor.

Jack and Silas walked over to Marlene's desk to see what was going on. The driver of the sedan stepped out; she was a pale brunette with almost elf-like features. She wore yoga pants and a tank top, and in Jack's opinion, she wore them flawlessly.

The woman walked toward their building and hesitated as she glanced at the different storefronts squeezed side by side. "Bet she'll go frozen yogurt," Silas said, referring to the shop next door. But instead the woman walked straight for their office. Jack and Silas both stepped back from Marlene's desk and tried to look casual as the woman entered.

"Looks like you got some car problems," Marlene said.

"I'm afraid so," the woman said. "So sorry to bother you, but does anyone here know anything about overheating engines?"

Jack stepped forward, but Silas jumped in front of him. "Sure," Silas said, "let's go take a look."

"Great," the woman said. "If you both wouldn't mind looking at it, I'd be so grateful. I'm Fleming, by the way." She held out her delicate hand, and they both shook it in turn.

"You just come from yoga?" Marlene asked.

"Yes," said Fleming. She pointed south. "That new place down the road from here... I can't remember what it's called."

"Reach for the Sky?"

"That's the place," Fleming said, and turned to leave.

"You like it?"

She stopped at the door. "Yes. Very much."

"I'm looking for a new place," Marlene said. "I got kicked out of my regular studio."

Fleming already seemed to be finished with the conversation, but she forced enough politeness to ask, "Why's that?"

"I got in a fight with my yoga instructor. Like, actual fistfighting." She shadowboxed a few punches to illustrate.

"Okay, Marlene," Jack said, noting Fleming's impatience. "We'll be right back. Try not to knock out any clients while we're gone."

By the time they popped the hood on the sedan, the steam was already dissipating. "Oh yeah," Silas said, looking under the hood at nothing in particular. "Probably a blown head gasket."

Jack spotted something, leaned in and reached behind the

engine block. He pulled out a yellow cap. "Surge tank cap," Jack said. "It must have been loose, or somebody didn't put it on all the way."

Silas nodded. "Sure, could be that, too."

"I just had my oil changed this morning," Fleming said. "They did a whole fluid check thing. I'll bet they didn't put it back on. Thank you so much."

"No problem. Exact same thing happened to me probably ten years ago."

"Nice to know I'm not the only one with that kind of luck," she said with a half-smile. "So the car's going to be fine, right? Do I just need to put some more coolant in it?"

"You should probably let it sit for awhile and cool off before you do anything," Jack said.

"Then how about I buy you lunch?" she said. "Anywhere within walking distance."

"Okay, you two have fun," Silas said, backing up toward the office. He did it slowly, just in case there might still be an invitation for him, too. There wasn't.

As soon as he walked back inside, Marlene said, "She's a liar."

"Huh?"

"There's no way she just came from yoga."

"How do you know?"

"Reach for the Sky only does hot yoga on Tuesdays," she said.

"Hot, as in sexy?" he asked. "Because I just might have to sign up if that's the kind of clientele they draw."

"No, hot, as in, work out for ninety minutes in a room that's a hundred and five degrees. It's not humanly possible to come out looking like she did, all clean and fresh."

"Maybe she showered," he said.

"She was wearing her workout clothes. Which, by the way, had no sweat stains. And her hair wasn't wet. Trust me, if her hair got wet in this humidity, it would stay wet for the rest of the day."

"But why would she lie about that?"

"I don't know," said Marlene. "But I don't trust her. Maybe she's some kind of scammer. Whatever you do, don't let Jack give her any money."

Down the street, Jack and Fleming ended up at Doc's, a former repair garage turned burger and beer joint. The place retained its roll-up garage bay doors and industrial decor, but gave off a warm and friendly vibe that Jack hoped would put him at ease in the presence of a female companion. After all, it had been a while.

"So," she said. "Roundabout Design. You a fan of British motorways?"

Jack smiled. "My ex-wife and I went to Europe for our honeymoon," he said. "In England, I was so tickled by the word 'roundabout.' Here, people say it as a sort of rough measure of time. Like, 'I'll be finished with work 'round about six, so we could meet for dinner after that.'"

"Oh, could we?" Fleming said, amused. "How about we finish lunch first."

"I didn't mean... I was just... anyway." He felt his face flush. "Point is, I liked the duality of the word. Plus, I always feel like I end up taking the long way around with just about everything I do."

"I know that feeling," she said.

"So what do you do?" he asked.

"I manage housekeeping at a little place near downtown."

"Oh? What's it called?"

"I'm sure you've never heard of it. It's pretty small." Pause. "Nexus," she said.

"So is it like a bed and breakfast type of place?"

"You could say that."

As they talked, Jack made mental notes of every scrap of personal info he got. She was thirty-five, divorced, no kids. She did yoga twice a week, but wished she could do more. When Jack recounted his saga about becoming a presidential elector, she listened and smiled, but in the end just shrugged and said, "I can't say I know much about politics." She had a cat named Flannery, after Flannery O'Connor. She was working on a novel, but wasn't far enough along to let anyone see it.

At nearly every opportunity, though, she steered the conversation back to Jack. She seemed especially curious about his family and his ex-wife.

"It sounds like your marriage was pretty great most of the time," she said. "Do you ever have any regrets?"

The question struck him as odd at first. She wanted to know if he still had feelings for his ex-wife. But this was probably a common topic in the dating realm, of which he knew nothing. It made sense for a woman to protect herself from getting involved with someone who's still hung up on his former spouse.

"I'm sure there are all sorts of things I could've done differently," Jack said. "Been a better listener, offer more encouragement for her career... all that stuff. And I imagine she'd say the same. But you know what I regret most?"

"What?"

"Letting her keep the dog."

Fleming smiled. "Must've been some dog."

"He was. Is. His name is Satch. He's a Great Pyrenees. Magnificent white beast, nearly a hundred pounds. Gentle as a dove."

"How did she end up with him?"

"Since she was going to be living alone when we separated, I figured it would be better for her to have a giant ghost dog to keep intruders away. Even if he would never actually hurt anyone, a hundred-pound dog is a pretty good deterrent."

"Why don't you get another one?"

"I know this is weird, but... just knowing he's out there, I'd kind of feel like I was cheating on him." Fleming raised a brow but said nothing. "I know it sounds stupid," he said. "He probably wouldn't even remember me if he saw me now."

"I doubt that," she said, swirling her iced tea with her straw but never taking her eyes off him. "You're pretty memorable."

28

The NEXT MORNING when Jack arrived at the office, Silas was wearing a lecherous grin.

"You never answered my texts last night," Silas said, "so I assume you were..." He giggled. "Occupied."

"Silas, stop being creepy," Marlene said. She reached into the mini-fridge below her desk and handed Jack a small bottle of pomegranate juice. "So did you have a good time?" she asked.

"We did. Very enjoyable dinner."

"And?" Silas asked.

"Great conversation."

"And?"

"And," Jack said, "any additional details are beyond the purview of this particular confabulation, good sir."

"I don't know what any of that means, but I'm pretty sure you used the word 'perv' in there, so I'm just going to let my mind run with that."

"You had sex," Marlene said. "Just say it so he'll stop."

Jack stayed silent, but he could not conceal his smile. "Wow," said Silas. "On the first day you met her. Right out the gate."

"When are you seeing her again?" asked Marlene.

"Tonight," Jack said. "I have to say, she really seems to know what she wants."

"Yeah," said Silas, "but what she wants is you, so I think it's only fair to question her judgment."

"I guess this means you're finally over whats-her-face," Marlene said. "So at least there's that."

"You guys don't have to avoid saying her name in front of me. She's not some sorceress whose name holds magic, evil powers."

"Fine," said Marlene. "Anna."

Jack took a gulp of juice, swirled it around in his mouth as he thought it over. "Yeah, let's stick with whats-her-face."

"Do me a favor," Silas said, putting a hand on Jack's shoulder. "Take it slow with this girl. You haven't been out there for a while, so let me tell you: it's rough. You might think you're going out with a mild-mannered soccer mom, but then you find out later she's a meth-addicted webcam porn star who happens to be transgender."

"I still don't know how you didn't figure that one out sooner," Marlene said.

"It was a very deep tuck. My point is, people are not always what they seem."

"In other words," said Jack, "there's no way this could be a normal, beautiful woman who just happens to like me."

"Based on my experience," Silas said, "odds are against it."

"If I ever give you even just a hint that I might use your experience as the basis for any life decisions, please shoot me in the face."

"I know you don't think I'm serious. But I'm just saying... be careful."

Marlene spun around in her chair to face Jack. "You know I hate nothing more than agreeing with Silas," she said, "but it's true. You're basically a delicate little orchid when it comes to dating."

"Fine. Noted," Jack said, and went into his office, shutting the door a little harder than usual.

A note on his desk told him to call Vera Lynn. He dialed. "I put you down for steaks," she said.

"Steaks for what?"

"For the Club's Labor Day barbecue."

"Oh, yeah," Jack said. "Steaks. Sure. You think it would be okay if I... brought someone?"

"You're pretty much the guest of honor since you got elector. I'm sure you can do whatever." Pause. "You talking about a girl?"

"Yeah. A pretty great one too."

"I've heard that before. Look what happened last time."

"Trust me," he said. "I don't think you'll have a problem with this one."

29

W<small>HEN</small> F<small>LEMING GOT BACK</small> to the Nexus that morning, she debriefed the team. "I don't think we'll have a problem with this one," she said.

"What are his exploitables?" Langhorne asked.

"Definitely not the ex-wife," Fleming said. "Although he's got a soft spot for the dog she kept."

"So what does that leave us?" asked Miles. "Dognapping?"

"No animals at risk," Vig said. His expression told everyone in the room that there would be no further discussion on the matter.

"This guy's father still looms pretty large in his life, right?" asked Grant.

Fleming nodded. "He's the reason Jack went after the elector slot-"

"Jack?" Candace interrupted. "He's Jack now?"

"What would you like me to call him?" Fleming asked.

"How about Patton? Or just 'the target'?"

Grant spoke up to break the awkwardness. "I asked about the father because we turned up some pretty good stuff on him. If Patton's doing this in memory of his father, maybe we can leak some damaging info and he'll be so ashamed that he'll bow out."

"Or he'll want to turn against everything his father stood for," Candace said. "In which case, he should be easy to flip."

"I still think my plan is the way to go," Fleming said. "He's already attached to me, and that'll just get stronger. If he thinks I'm in danger, he'll do whatever we want."

"I like Grant's plan," Candace said. "It's the first one I've heard in weeks that doesn't involve threats or violence."

"We can try Grant's plan," Langhorne said. "And if it doesn't work, we still have Fleming in place. Is everyone happy now?"

"Fine," Fleming said.

"When are you supposed to see him again?" asked Langhorne.

"Tonight."

"You don't think that's suspicious?" Candace asked. "That your schedule is suddenly clear for this guy you just met?"

"No, I don't. And this isn't exactly my first rodeo, so I'd appreciate a little less second-guessing."

"Enough," Langhorne said. "Miles, let's also get going on the cyber front. Anything you can do to mess with this guy's business and personal life. Just don't make it look conspicuous."

Miles gave him a salute, pulled his keyboard into his lap, and started typing.

Langhorne studied the board that listed the electors. "Platt, where are we on Atchison?"

"I just got the video. We're headed over there now."

Gerald Atchison lived in New Braunfels, between Austin and San Antonio. The home appeared nothing more than a modest single-story from the street, but it backed up to a priceless personal slice of waterfront along the Guadalupe River.

Atchison invited Platt and Vig into his study and closed the door. Platt and Atchison sat; Vig chose to stand, which clearly unnerved Atchison.

"What exactly can I do for you gentlemen?" he asked. "On the phone you said you were looking for a vacation home in the area, but I'm getting a different vibe now."

"Very perceptive," said Platt. "This is why you're so successful dealing with people. We actually have an offer for you. But first, tell me: do you watch the international news?"

"I stay informed," Atchison said, confused by the direction of the conversation.

"Did you hear about those machete attacks in Nigeria? Muslims slaughtering Christians in the street." Platt shook his head. "Awful stuff. I certainly wouldn't want to be there right now."

Atchison just glared at Platt and said nothing.

"Oh I'm sorry," Platt said. "I forgot about your daughter. Ashley, is it? She's over there right now on a mission, isn't she? Helping to build a church. How is she? Have you heard from her recently?"

Atchison sat up in his chair. "If you lay a finger-" Vig pushed him back down—with a single finger, perhaps to prove a point.

"See, that's the thing about developing nations on the other side of the world," Platt said, pulling out his phone and tapping the screen. "You just can't trust the rule of law like you can here. You have to rely on corrupt police or military commanders for protection. And trust me when I say that they can be bought with shockingly small amounts of money."

Platt showed Atchison the screen. It was a dark, grainy video of a young blonde girl sitting in what looked like a church pew. Was she praying? No... her hands were tied together. Standing over her was a soldier with an AK-47 gripped tightly in his hands. Even with the shaky camera, it was easy to see that she was sobbing.

"Since you're so good at reading people," Platt said, "I don't need to tell you that this is the face of someone who fears for her life."

Atchison's expression went blank. "I'll do it. Whatever it is you want. I'll do it."

30

"Do you know why our website is down?" Marlene asked as soon as Jack got to the office the next morning. He was late, but still earlier than Silas.

"I didn't even know it *was* down," Jack said. "Call the hosting company."

"I did. Nobody answered so I left a message."

"Well, that's about all you can do then."

"And did you know we've got, like, five super-negative reviews on the local business ratings site?"

"Really?" Jack couldn't imagine five different clients that were unhappy with his work. He'd only ever had one real complaint; the guy didn't know what he wanted, and after Jack tried three different approaches on spec, the guy still complained. "What do they say?" he asked.

"Inferior art, slow to deliver, does not handle criticism well..."

"What a bunch of lying bastards."

"I don't think that helps your argument on that last one."

"What I mean is, these aren't real clients," Jack said. "There's no way. How can they do that?"

"It's the Internet," Marlene said. "They can do anything."

Jack skimmed the reviews. All of them indicated some knowledge of his business—location, office setup, employees—but none of them provided enough detail to be identified as specific clients. His stomach suddenly felt uneasy. What if even just *one* of these reviews was legitimate?

"Does anyone actually look at these?" Jack asked. "To choose where to do business?"

"Seems like mostly old people who just shuffled their way online. But anybody could turn this stuff up with just a web search."

"Could you look into disputing or removing those?" Jack asked.

"Sure, after I do some of my real work." She clicked her mouse and the screen filled with an elaborate black and white graphic.

"What's that?"

"It's for a record store downtown," Marlene said. "The guy wanted a logo that was inspired by a tattoo he's got on his wrist." She clicked again, and her screen displayed a photo of the tattooed wrist.

"Wow," Jack said. "That's really good."

She shrugged. "It's getting there."

"Looks like you've done just fine without me around all the time."

"Yeah, well, you basically abandoned me these past few

months, so it was pretty much sink or swim."

"Which forced you to grow and adapt. You're welcome."

"Jerk," she said, and threw a foam stress ball at Jack's face.

He went to his office and sank into his chair. There was a padded envelope on his desk. As he reached for it, something fell from the ceiling and splashed next to him. That was when he noticed the brown puddle next to his computer. He looked up, and saw that the ceiling tile above his desk was so saturated with dark brown liquid that it was drooping in the center.

"Marlene! What the hell is this... stuff in my office?"

Marlene peeked in. "What? I didn't mess with anything in here. I don't even go in here except to put your mail on your desk. You're welcome, by the way."

Jack pointed at the ceiling. She looked up and crinkled her face. "Yuck," she said. "I guess that's what's been smelling so weird."

"Do you remember who's on the second floor above us?"

"I don't know. Maybe that plastic surgeon."

"Call the property manager and let him know." As an afterthought, he added, "Please."

When she left, he opened the padded envelope. Inside was a recordable DVD with the words "Honor thy father?" written across it in black marker. Jack slid the disc into his computer's drive and a video file started playing.

On the screen, in grainy black-and-white, was his father.

The video was shot from a low, odd angle, probably about waist high. It was clear that Ray had no idea he was being filmed. Judging by his father's appearance and vigor, the video must have been shot at least five years before, and probably more. Ray was seated at a table in what was probably the coffee shop just off the square in Nobles. In the edge of the frame, Jack could see the arm of another man—the person doing the secret filming. He couldn't identify it, but then he heard the voice:

"I got hold of some mighty interesting information, Ray." The voice was younger, less grizzled, but Jack could tell right away who the speaker was: Sheriff Hil Sempel, probably back when he was still Deputy Hil Sempel.

Onscreen, Ray said, "I got biscuits waiting, so just keep talking while I eat." He tore a biscuit in half and dragged it through a puddle of gravy.

"By the way, Waylon says hello," Hil said. "From up Gatesville."

Ray just kept eating.

"For a long time," Hil said, "I wondered how it was that my brother got sent up as an adult for boosting that car, but his two idiot friends got off as juvies and never did time."

Ray jabbed a biscuit toward Hil, slopping gravy on the table. "You best get up, turn around, and walk out of here before you finish that thought."

"Ten thousand dollars," Hil said.

"Is that supposed to mean something?"

"You know exactly what it means. And it's the answer to my question about why those other two boys never went to jail."

Ray wiped gravy from the corner of his mouth. "They said your brother was the ringleader."

"I'll bet they did," said Hil.

"Anyway, I don't know anything about ten thousand dollars."

"That's a shame." Hil leaned forward, just enough that his cheek poked into view on the screen. He lowered his voice, and it was barely audible on the recording. "Say, you remember my aunt Connie? Works down the bank?"

Ray just stared, silent.

"She might could help you remember about that money," Hil said.

"What is it you're looking for?" Ray asked. "Your brother ain't coming out early unless it's on good behavior. Nothing I can do about that."

"Maybe there's something you can do for *me*."

"What's that?" Ray asked.

A hand drifted in front of the lens, and a moment later, the picture went to static.

31

VERA LYNN WATCHED the video on Jack's laptop, and when it finished, she walked to the front bay window and stared silently at a group of neighborhood children playing in the street.

"Did you know about this?" Jack asked.

Vera Lynn sighed. "What do you want me to say, Jack?"

"I want the truth," Jack said.

"I don't know anything about money. I didn't take over Daddy's books till two years ago."

"What about the rest?"

"I remember when Waylon got sentenced. His two friends got off easy, and there was a lot of talk about that. They testified that Waylon was behind it all, and it was two against one, so that was that. But folks that know those kids said Waylon was a follower, and that was my feeling too.

"The dumb thing was, if they'd stolen Mrs. Damp's Pinto

across the street instead of that fancy SUV, he would've been out in six months. As it was, he got six years. I thought Daddy came down hard on him with sentencing, but he never said why. I figured he felt bad about it after, because he stood with Hil for County Sheriff some months later."

"He endorsed Hil for Sheriff," Jack said. "That's the favor Hil's talking about in the video."

"Could be so," Vera Lynn admitted.

"Which means he really did take a bribe. Otherwise he would've told Hil to go pound sand. No way Dad would've helped out someone who falsely accused him of something like that."

"What's your point, Jack? He's dead. You want me to go dig him up so you can smack his skeleton around a while?"

"I've been listening to everybody talk about what a great man he was, how he was a pillar of the community, and I've just thanked them and agreed with them. You knew him better than anybody, so you tell me: which one was he? Pillar of the community or corrupt scumbag?"

"He was a man, just like you. You're the one that magnified him, built him into some mythical thing."

"After everything I've gone through to honor his memory-"

"Oh please," Vera Lynn said. "You can use that line about how this elector thing is all for honoring Daddy on other folks, and hell, I'll even help you sell it. But don't try that baloney on me. I know what you're really after."

"What?"

"Forgiveness. For the way you treated him the last few years."

Jack wanted to argue, but couldn't. "He was hard on me

too."

"Yes, he was," Vera Lynn said. "Both of you were always so much alike that you refused to see it in each other."

"I honestly don't know if I can do this," Jack said. "This whole elector thing. Everyone wants to hear about how I'm doing this as a tribute to a great man. I don't know what to say about him anymore."

"He's the same man he was yesterday," Vera Lynn said. "You're the only one that's different."

Jack got up to leave. "You better find someone else to bring steaks," he said. "I'm sure as hell not spending my Labor Day blowing smoke up the collective ass of Nobles about the great and honorable Ray Patton."

*   *   *

"So that's the story," Jack said. Fleming lay across the couch with her head in his lap. An empty wine bottle sat on its side next to his foot. They were at his place, of course... always his place.

He brushed her hair back and tucked it behind her ear. "What do you think?" he asked.

"Pretty crazy," she said.

"But do you think I should quit? As an elector?"

"Is that what they're trying to get you to do?" she asked.

"Who?"

Fleming's face froze for a fleeting moment. "The people who sent you the video," she said. "Whoever that is. They must have had a reason for sending it, right?"

It had never occurred to Jack that the video might be in

any way related to him being an elector. The thought that someone was trying to manipulate him into quitting—and even worse, make it seem like it was his own idea—left him feeling defiant.

"Why would somebody want me to quit? Why would anybody care?"

"I haven't the slightest idea," she said. "Don't even listen to me. I'm a little drunk."

"I'm not quitting," he decided. "I made my dad a promise, and I'm going to keep it. Even if he doesn't deserve it."

"Good," Fleming said. She lifted her head and kissed the underside of his chin. "That's what I was going to say too."

"I gotta pee," he said, and she leaned forward to let him up. As soon as he closed the bathroom door, she pulled out her phone.

"It's me," she said. "Patton's not dropping out." Pause. "Certain. Tell them to move ahead."

32

When Jack arrived at the office, Marlene whispered excitedly, "There's someone waiting in your office."

"Who?"

She shrugged. "She said you were expecting her."

Jack couldn't think of anyone he might be expecting. Perhaps it was someone from the insurance company, wanting to check out the ceiling damage from Doctor Frankenstein's leaky drainage upstairs.

When Jack entered his office, the woman stood and shook his hand. "Mister Patton, it's a pleasure."

"Please, call me Jack." He invited her to sit once more, and took his own seat behind his desk. The one word that came to mind when he looked at her was "sharp." Neatly dressed, perfectly featured, friendly and confident.

"My name is Candace," she said. "And I'm here to make your life a whole lot better."

"You're not selling one of those nutrition programs, are you?"

She shook her head. "I'm not selling anything. With any luck, I'm buying."

"You need some design work done?"

"Nothing like that," she said. "How's business, by the way?"

"We keep busy."

"I think you're putting on a brave face."

"Meaning?"

"You've only had two clients in the past month," she said. "And the bad news is that things are going to get worse."

"How did you-"

"The medical waste leak in your ceiling? The one that's completely not your fault in any way? The property manager is going to serve papers on you tomorrow. He's suing you for negligence."

"For what? Being dumb enough to lease an office underneath a plastic surgeon?"

"He claims that you should have noticed the problem sooner, and by not reporting it to him, you compounded the damage it caused."

"That's ridiculous," said Jack.

"Yes it is," she said. "But that doesn't change the fact that you'll have to waste your time, energy, and money to defend yourself against some jerk who doesn't want to take responsibility himself."

"I don't understand. Are you just here to ruin my day?"

Candace lifted her briefcase up to her lap. "What if I told you I could take care of all these problems?"

"How would you do that?"

"I think a million dollars would be a good start," she said.

Jack laughed. "Sure. And what would I have to do for a million dollars?"

"Cast one vote," she said.

Jack waited for some elaboration, but none was forthcoming. "I don't understand," he said.

"It's simple. You are a presidential elector. When you're called to cast your vote in December, you vote for the current president instead of Governor Randell."

"But Randell's going to win. Probably the whole thing, but Texas for sure."

"Yes."

"So why would I do that?" As soon as he said it, the answer came to him. "Oh. For a million dollars."

Candace opened the briefcase and turned it toward him. It held stacks of hundred dollar bills wrapped in paper bands. "This is just under half a million," she said. She pulled out a single stack and placed it on the desk. "That's ten thousand right now, just so you'll know we're serious. Not a bad deal, huh?"

"I can't do it," he said, pushing the stack of bills back to her. "I signed a pledge saying I would vote for the Republican nominee."

"That's not legally enforceable," she said. "Probably not in any state, but most certainly not in Texas. There are no laws against changing your vote as an elector."

"That doesn't sound true."

"Look it up for yourself. In practical terms, your contract with the Republican Party amounts to nothing more than a pinky swear. Even in the states that have laws binding electors, no one has ever been prosecuted for voting differently."

"Jeez, it's happened before? How many times?"

"There have been faithless electors in about twenty different presidential elections."

"Faithless electors," Jack repeated.

"That's what they're called. But don't worry... they've never affected the outcome of an election."

"So what's the point then?"

"Our purpose," Candace said, "is to send a message to the extremists within the party. We want them to think long and hard about drifting too far from the realm of common sense, from the things that most Americans agree on."

Jack couldn't deny the appeal of the pitch. Common sense was exactly what he felt was missing in politics nowadays. But he couldn't bring himself to entertain the thought. "You have to understand," he said, "I'm from Nobles. The people there are the ones that helped me get chosen as an elector. If I turned around and voted for a Democrat, I wouldn't be able to show my face there ever again."

"What if they didn't know?"

"Of course they'd know," said Jack. "Everybody knows who the electors vote for."

"Not in every state," Candace said. "And as of May, Texas now has a voter privacy law that grants electors the same secret ballot rights as every other voter. All they'd know is that one of the thirty-eight electors voted differently. And like I said, it's happened in more than a third of all the presidential elections in American history. Not exactly a big deal."

She had an answer for everything. Jack tried to think of other logical arguments against her proposal, but came up empty. A million dollars. Still, he kept picturing Vera Lynn's face, and thought about all the people in Nobles that had entrusted him to act as their mouthpiece.

As he struggled with the idea, Candace moved in to strike a decisive blow. "I know you're doing this to honor your father's memory," she said. "But don't you think he'd want you to look out for yourself and Vera Lynn? That's exactly what *he* was doing when he took that money."

Jack didn't need to ask what money she was talking about. Now he knew who had sent him the video. "No way," he said. "I won't do it. Find someone else."

Candace saw the grim determination in his face, and must have realized the opportunity was gone. She shrugged and slid a business card across his desk. In the center, in small, elegant type, was a single phone number. "You can always give me call if you change your mind," she said.

"I won't."

She stood to leave. "You're a decent man, Jack," she said. "Unfortunately, decency is not often rewarded in this world."

33

"Not responsive to monetary incentives," Candace said. Langhorne, Grant, and Miles watched as she erased the "$?" from next to Patton's name on the dry-erase board. It was a skeleton crew at the Nexus; Platt and Vig were out in the field, and Fleming was either with Jack or on her way to see him.

"Time to apply pressure then," said Langhorne.

"I'd still like to give it a few days," she said. "Just in case he comes around."

"Three days. Then Fleming gets her shot. Next item." Langhorne fired a laser pointer at the rightmost whiteboard. It showed a rough timeline of the operation. With his pointer, below "Election," he targeted the word "Scandal."

"We need a scandal for Randell. Grant?"

Grant flipped through some files with an uncertain look on his face. "I've been digging for weeks, and it's really just the same stuff as every other politician. Possible conflict of interest with his wife and the prescription medication bill he supported, since she's a doctor. He got a special home loan rate, but what politician hasn't. Plenty of contradictions in his voting record, but that doesn't really qualify as scandalous."

"It doesn't have to be true," Langhorne said. "It just has to have enough of a kernel of verifiable information that we can grow it into something huge. Something to really outrage his conservative base. It'll need to take at least a week for the whole thing to unravel. We'll release it a few days before the electors are called in December."

"How about a secret homosexual affair?" Candace offered.

"Done to death," Langhorne said.

"The guy's had more shell corporations than you can count," Grant said. "Probably some loose ends there that we could pick at."

"Good," said Langhorne. "Just make it big."

"If we're going to put Randell in the middle of a made-up scandal," Miles asked, "why not just do it right before the election? Maybe it'll sway voters."

"No, it won't," Langhorne said. "The point of this scandal isn't to change anyone's mind about Randell. The goal is to give our electors an excuse for flipping. If the electoral vote happens in the midst of an outrageous scandal, suddenly a bunch of faithless votes make a lot more sense."

"What if we say he used a shell corporation to traffic guns to Mexican drug lords?" Miles suggested.

"Good," Langhorne said. "But bigger."

"Rocket launchers to Islamic terrorists," said Grant.

"Now you're onto something. I want to see paper trails that all lead back to Randell. Emails from his personal accounts, dummied phone records, the works. Miles, you can get started on that. Grant and I have to go meet the courier for another cash pickup. I don't want to come back and find out you were playing video games the whole time we were gone."

Grant and Langhorne left; Candace and Miles were alone in the house. "Miles," said Candace, "I need you to access the GPS trackers on Grant's computer."

"I'm not allowed to touch Grant's stuff," he said. "That was made abundantly clear after someone—definitely not me—got peanut butter in his keyboard."

"His unit is the only one that can display the GPS info, right?"

"Yeah..."

"What happens if something goes wrong with the money pickup? How would we know where to find them?"

"Um..."

"Look, when Langhorne's not here, I'm the one in charge, right?"

"I... guess?"

"You won't get in trouble," Candace said. "I'll tell them that I ordered you to do it, for everyone's safety."

Miles sighed. "I don't have a choice, do I?"

Candace shook her head.

Grant's computer was locked down, but Miles had seen him enter his password out of the corner of his eye, and had an idea about which keys he pressed. "If this doesn't work," he said, "I'll need to run a cracker."

But Miles was being modest about his skills, and he got in on his second try.

"I'll take it from here," Candace said, and rolled him back

to his own desk.

The GPS tracking program showed each team member as a different-colored dot accompanied by a two-letter designation. Grant was represented by a purple dot with the letters "GI." According to the tracker, he was moving south along Interstate 35.

After Miles went back to his own work, Candace brought up Fleming's tracker, a red circle labeled "FC." She was currently at Jack's condo near Zilker Park. Candace switched to tracking history and scrolled backward through time, watching as the dot danced back and forth between the Nexus and Jack's place, then stayed mainly at the Nexus.

Then the map zoomed out, and Candace could see that Fleming made a trip to Gurston a few weeks before. She scrolled farther back in time, and saw the trip to west Texas just before the state convention. She checked both locations against the information in her files, just to be certain. Then she logged out of Grant's computer.

"I'll be back," she said to Miles, and headed out the door.

34

"Somebody's trying to get me to change my vote," Jack said.

"Vote for what?" asked Silas.

He looked around to make sure no one was listening. They were at Doc's, and the crowd seemed casual enough, but you never knew who might be sitting at the next table. "My vote in the electoral college," he said.

Silas laughed. "What, are they trying to get you to vote Democrat?"

Jack's expression remained grave, and Silas stopped laughing. "Holy shit," he said. "Seriously?"

Jack nodded.

"Why on earth would they want you to vote Democrat in Texas?"

"They said they wanted to send a message."

"Huh. Maybe the message is, 'Hey everybody, look how stupid the electoral college is.' In which case, I fully support it. So did they offer anything in the way of... compensation?"

Jack drew a deep breath. "A million dollars."

Silas nearly choked on his beer. "No way. This has got to be somebody yanking your chain, man."

"I saw the money. Well, about half of it. She tried to give me ten thousand, but I wouldn't take it."

"Dude, if this is real, you ought to take that money and run like a mofo. Do you know how far a million bucks would go in other parts of the world? You could live out your days like a king in Cambodia, or Bolivia, or Tajikistan..."

"I'm not moving to a foreign country. And I'm pretty sure you made that last one up, anyway."

"What's the matter? Don't want to leave behind the new girlfriend? Pack her up and take her with. Women love to travel."

"I cannot imagine why a romantic like you is still single. Anyway, I told them I wasn't interested. She gave me her card." He pulled it out and twirled it between his fingers.

Silas took the card, inspected it. "Are they just hoping you'll change your mind, or are they offering the million bucks to someone else? There's a lot of other electors out there to choose from."

"No idea."

"I'm telling you man, take the money. The whole system's rigged anyway. Might as well get what you can out of it."

"That's the kind of attitude that lets corruption spread," Jack said. "I'll be damned if I'm going to be a part of it." He spun his stool away from the table and got up.

"Don't worry, I'll get this round," Silas said as Jack walked out.

35

WHEN LANGHORNE AND GRANT returned to the Nexus, they found Miles energetically tapping away at his keyboard—a sure sign that he had been playing a video game, and had switched it off as soon as he saw their car pull up.

"Where's Candace?" Langhorne asked.

"I don't know. She said she'd be right back."

"How long ago was that?"

Miles squinted at the clock in the corner of his screen. "Jeez, like two hours ago."

Langhorne had Grant pull up the GPS tracker. He selected the yellow dot labeled "CW." It showed her current location as... the Nexus. Grant zoomed in. According to the tracker, she was just outside the house, near the driveway.

Langhorne and Grant walked back outside while Miles watched from the window. They searched the ground along the sidewalk and front lawn. Grant pointed hesitantly to the garbage can, next to the driveway. Langhorne lifted the lid and pulled out the tracker.

Miles ran back to his desk as Langhorne stormed through the front door. "Change all the passwords," he said, heading straight for his office. "Did she go near my office?" he asked Miles. When Miles hesitated, he repeated, louder: "Did she go near my office?"

"Um, no," Miles said. "Not that I saw."

"Do you think she was taken?" Grant asked.

"No," said Langhorne.

In his office, nothing appeared to be disturbed, but he double-checked everything anyway. As he searched through his drawers, his phone rang.

"You must think I'm an idiot," Candace said when he picked up. "And I was, too. I believed you."

"Would you like to clarify?" Langhorne asked.

"Of course you need clarification. Because obviously this wasn't the only time you lied to me."

"Exactly what is it you think you know?"

"Hubert. Vestry. She killed them both."

After a long pause, Langhorne asked, "Where are you?"

"You will never see me again," she said. "If you send anyone for me, they will not come back alive."

"Come on now, Candace," he said. "You're a lover, not a fighter."

"You repulse me," she said. "I thought I convinced you to do this the right way. But you're always going to do what you're going to do, no matter what, aren't you?"

He leaned back in his chair. "When you need to make the numbers work, you find a way."

"It didn't have to be *that* way."

He brought up the footage from the security cameras he installed in the front rooms of the house. He rewound to the moment Candace got up and left. "When this whole thing is over, I will find you. You must know that. Loose ends have to be trimmed, for everyone's sake."

"You're welcome to try," she said, and hung up.

36

It was not yet six in the morning when Jack heard a knock at his door. Fleming moaned as he slid out of bed, but he kissed her hand and whispered, "Go back to sleep. I'll be right back."

Jack opened the door to find Silas and Marlene standing on the landing. Neither looked like they had gotten much sleep, if any at all.

"What's going on?" he asked.

"I think I figured it out," Silas said.

The two came inside. Silas took a seat on the couch in the living room, but Marlene stayed back, sitting at the dining table where Fleming's purse rested.

"What did you figure out?"

Silas looked Jack squarely in the eye. "Do you know how much money is spent on presidential campaigns?" he asked.

"Lots, I would guess," Jack said.

"Billions," Silas answered. "And they're spending more every single election. So a million is nothing to them." He leaned in closer to Jack. "I don't think your filthy rich friends are trying to send a message."

"What are they doing, then?"

"I'm pretty sure," Silas said, "that they're trying to steal the election."

"Really," was all Jack could think to say. Silas was being deadly serious, but over the years, Jack had heard too many crazy conspiracy theories from Silas to take them all seriously. Silas often leapt to the most outrageous conclusion possible— a sort of anti-Occam's Razor.

"I've been up all night researching this," he said, then remembered Marlene. "I mean we. And it's the only thing that makes sense. Think about it: if you can flip one elector, why stop there?"

"So you don't think it's just me?"

Silas shook his head. "If they're already thinking like this, I don't see why they'd stop at just you. There have been groups of electors that have conspired in other elections. In 1836, a bunch of electors from Virginia made a stink and refused to elect the Democratic Party's candidate for vice president because he had a relationship with a female slave, who, by the way, was a grand total of one-eighth black. But the guy was elected by the Senate anyway. Still, my point is, the idea's not as crazy as it sounds."

Jack was starting to get a sick feeling in his stomach. As much as he tried to convince himself otherwise, Silas was presenting a coherent argument. He looked over to Marlene, who had her hands under the table messing around with a phone. "You buying this?" he asked.

She looked up as if she'd been caught in the middle of something, but quickly switched to her usual apathetic demeanor. "I wouldn't put it past them," she said. "Look at the other crap that politicians try all the time to get votes."

"From a purely financial perspective," said Silas, "it would be one of the cheapest ways to win a presidential election. Think about it: how many electoral votes do you need to win the election?"

"Two hundred and seventy," Jack said without hesitation.

"Right on the money," Silas said, impressed. "You're not as hopeless as I thought. Okay, so imagine if someone paid off two hundred and seventy electors with a million dollars each. That's still less money than was spent in each of the last six presidential elections. Way cheaper than buying ad time, hiring canvassers..."

"You wouldn't need to pay them *all* off," Jack said, reluctantly seeing the logic behind the idea. "Not if you're talking about a Democrat or Republican candidate. Because either way, almost half the people are going to vote for them anyway."

"Exactly," Silas said. "You gotta figure that New York, California, states like that are going to go for the Democrat, and states like Texas are bound to swing Republican. So maybe you only need to buy, say, thirty electoral votes. Because a flipped vote is twice as powerful."

"How do you mean?"

"There are always a fixed number of electors, and they all have to vote for somebody. If you're flipping an elector, it takes a vote away from the other guy, and gives the vote to your guy. So if the electoral count would have been 240 to

298, and you swing thirty votes, you just eliminated a fifty-eight vote lead and beat the other guy by two votes—270 to 268. And that's only thirty million bucks right there."

"Why Texas, though? Talk about your diehard Republicans..."

"That's exactly why. No one would expect it. And they know for a fact Texas will vote Republican. It's the biggest guaranteed pile of Republican electoral votes in the country."

"Do you really think so many electors would be willing to sell their vote? These are usually the most trusted people in their party."

Silas's expression turned grave. "People have done much worse for much less."

"I guess," Jack said. "But I just can't imagine."

"And it might not just be bribes. It could be blackmail, threats... we have no idea." Considering his own words, Silas asked, "They didn't threaten you, did they?"

"No."

"Good. But I wouldn't just assume that they're done with you."

Jack thought the whole theory through. "I'm still not buying it," he said. "You'd need to have so many pieces in place, somebody would say something. How could it be worth all that trouble?"

"The prize is choosing the leader of the free world," Silas said. "I'd say that's worth all kinds of trouble."

Fleming appeared in the hallway in one of Jack's t-shirts, luminous despite her unkempt hair.

"Morning," Silas said.

"Sorry," said Jack. "Were we too loud?"

She shook her head. "I should take a shower and get going," she said. She walked over to the dining table where Marlene sat and picked up her purse, then disappeared down the hall again.

"We should go," Marlene said.

Silas stood. "Just think it over. See if it doesn't make perfect sense."

Once Silas and Marlene were outside, he said, "Did you get it done?"

"Just barely," she said. "I'll need to test it and make sure it's working."

"Good. Let's go find out what this girl's really up to."

37

THE MORE JACK THOUGHT about what Silas said, the more he couldn't deny that the theory fit the available facts like a glove. But he still wasn't sure what to do with the information. He decided to consult with someone who had much more experience dealing with electors and the problems they might face.

"Someone's trying to steal the presidential election," Eleanor Craddock said. "In Texas."

"Yes," said Jack. "Maybe. I think so." Her office seemed so much colder, and the desk so much larger, than the last time he was here. Every time he opened his mouth, he felt like the words tumbled out and landed with a dead thud on that massive expanse of oak between them, never quite reaching her on the other side.

Eleanor sat back and stared down the length of her nose at him. "Do you remember what I told you last time you were here?" she asked. "About loyalty to the Party, and the highly selective process we use to choose our presidential electors?"

"Of course."

"Let's just suppose you could somehow explain why on Earth a bunch of Democrats would come to Texas to try and steal the presidential election. I don't think you can, but let me just spot you that one for now. Even if I believed that was happening, there's no way that our chosen electors would ever betray the party and vote Democrat. No... way."

"I can't say whether or not they've already approached other electors, but it would seem-"

"I guarantee you if somebody went to our other electors with this kind of nonsense, I'd have a line at my door. I've been knowing some of these people for thirty years or more. What you've got is some kind of crackpot pulling your leg, hoping to get a rise. Just ignore him and he'll go away."

Jack tried to put the pieces together in his head. Maybe she was right; if others were being solicited, surely word would have gotten out. Then a thought occurred to him, and he said it out loud: "What if they're blackmailing or threatening the other electors? That could be why no one's said anything."

"So now you think every other elector but you has got some deep, dark secret that's going to allow some stranger to hold their vote hostage." She threw her hands into the air, surrendering.

"Mister Patton, out of all our electors, you have—by far— the least amount of history and experience with the party. I've already gotten an earful from some people who think it's a mistake to put this kind of responsibility in your hands. If they heard you talking about some mysterious people trying to sway your vote, they'd be inclined to think that *you* are the one stirring the pot."

"I'm not a pot stirrer," Jack said, putting his hand to his chest as a pledge. "Really. I'm the guy who doesn't even touch the pot. I'm not even in the kitchen. I'm just telling you what happened. I may not know for sure why it happened, but it did."

Eleanor pursed her lips. "Well. Assuming this is true, I doubt you'll ever hear from this crazy person again. But if you do, call the police and tell them you're being harassed or something. Don't mention that you're an elector, because the last thing we want is media attention turning molehills into mountains and making everyone's job harder."

She lowered her head and looked at him over the top of her glasses; he could practically feel the intense heat of her naked stare. "And if I hear you've been talking to reporters or anybody else about this," she said, "mark my words: I'll boot you so fast your ass'll leave skid marks down Congress Avenue."

38

"Jack?" The voice was quavering, anxious.

"Fleming? What's wrong?"

"These people... they took me." She sounded like she was choking back tears. "I don't know where I am."

"Who took you?"

"They said they need your vote. What does that mean? Do you know them?"

"I'm going to call the police," said Jack.

"Noooooo!" she cried. "They said they'll kill me if you do."

"Tell them I'll vote however they want. But they have to let you go first."

"They said they won't. Not until after you vote."

Jack pressed the phone hard to his ear, trying to hear anything in the background that might reveal her location. All he could hear was static. "What can you see?" he asked. "Are you in a hotel room, a warehouse, what?"

"They won't let me-"

The line went dead.

Jack's mind was buzzing. Silas was right. There was far more to this than just sending a message to party leaders. He had to find Fleming. But where to start? Who could he call? Not the police, obviously. He dialed Silas, and before he could even form his words into coherent sentences, Silas said calmly, "Come to the office. We have to show you something."

When Jack got there, Silas cut off his frazzled attempt to explain the crisis. "Listen to me, buddy. The good news is that Fleming is okay."

"No! They kidnapped her and they're holding her hostage so I'll vote like they want."

"No they're not," said Silas. "Like I said, she's just fine, and I'll show you in a second."

"What are you talking about?" asked Jack. "How do you know?" He was suddenly paranoid. Was Silas somehow involved?

Silas grasped him by the shoulders. "To explain how I know this, we're going to have to transition away from the good news portion of the conversation. So please, promise you won't get mad."

Jack's expression darkened. "Tell me how you know."

Silas ushered him to Marlene's desk, where she was using a computer program Jack had never seen. "What's this?" he asked.

"It's a program that lets you listen in on another person's phone calls and read their text messages," Marlene answered. She clicked on a log entry, and Fleming's desperate call played.

Jack heard Fleming's terrified voice again. His throat

clenched up. "How did you-"

"I installed spyware on her phone," Marlene said, bracing herself for his response. "That morning we came over."

Jack just blinked, shell-shocked. "You were spying on my girlfriend?"

"Technically, yes," Marlene said. "But we only did it because we didn't trust her."

"How could you do that? What reason..." Jack couldn't absorb the extent of the betrayal. It was just too much to process.

"It's my fault," Silas said, shielding Marlene from the inevitable fallout. "I made her do it. The truth is, I was jealous that Fleming picked you over me, and I couldn't get over it. I convinced myself that she must be running some kind of scam. I'm sorry. The truth is, I'm just a sad, petty, jealous, little man."

Jack knew there would be consequences for what Silas had done, but he couldn't think about that yet. "How do you know she's okay?"

"This call was placed right after she talked to you," Marlene said. She clicked another log entry, and Fleming's voice played once more, but this time perfectly calm and assured:

"Patton's on the hook."

"Do you think he'll follow through?" The other voice was male, older. Jack had never heard it before.

"Oh yeah. He'd do anything for me."

"Perfect. That locks twenty."

"I might have a problem, though. My phone battery is draining really fast. Maybe it's the heat, but I don't know."

Pause. "Did you leave it unattended?"

"No," she said. "Well... Patton's friends came over early in the morning a couple days ago. It might have been vulnerable for a few minutes before I was able to get dressed and grab it."

"Don't come back here, then. We can't risk it. I'll send Miles to your location to take a look."

"Looks like there's an insurance office on the third floor. I'll wait up there."

The call ended, and it took Jack several seconds to wrap his brain around what he had heard.

"She's in on it," he said.

"Yeah."

"She wasn't kidnapped."

"No."

Jack felt unmoored, adrift. Was there anyone he could trust anymore? "Wait," he said. "How do we know she wasn't forced to say that last stuff? They could've had her at gunpoint."

Silas just shrugged, though he was visibly doubtful. "It's possible, I guess."

"We need to find her," Jack said. "She said she's somewhere with an insurance office on the third floor. There must be a way to narrow that down."

"I can do better," Marlene said. She clicked to a different menu and brought up a GPS tracker.

"How did you learn all this?" asked Jack.

"I used it on my ex-boyfriend, who turned out to be a lying, cheating a-hole." She clicked a few keys, and a map came up. "Unfortunately, he was also my yoga instructor."

The GPS revealed her location to be near the intersection of Fifth Street and Guadalupe.

"How long ago was that last call?" asked Jack.

"Five minutes or so."

He studied the GPS map for a few seconds, then bolted for the door. Silas went after him.

*   *   *

They found the building right away, and parked in an attached underground structure. Jack sprinted up the stairs to the third floor, not wanting to wait for the elevator. Silas reluctantly followed, and was wheezing by the time they came out of the stairwell.

"You go that way," Jack said, pointing to a hall of office suites on one side, "and I'll go this way."

Jack jogged down the hall, glancing into each office as he passed. She might not even still be there, he knew. But it was the only shot he had at finding out the truth.

When he got near the end of the hall, he heard someone yelling from behind him, where he had started. He ran back and caught a glimpse of Fleming and a young man with long hair running into the stairwell. Silas was following close behind.

"It's her!" he shouted, and disappeared through the stairwell door.

By the time Jack caught up, Fleming and the other man were nowhere to be found. Silas lay at the bottom of the flight of stairs, his left leg bent in a way that made Jack's stomach queasy. Jack ran down the stairs to Silas.

"Are you okay? Can you move your limbs?"

"Your girlfriend kicks like a mule," Silas said, scowling in pain. "Or maybe a ninja. A ninja mule."

"Hold still," said Jack. "I'll call an ambulance."

*　　　　　　*　　　　　　*

The x-ray showed three fractures in one leg, and one in the other. The doctor said that Silas would be confined to bed for several weeks.

"So I guess now we know for sure that she's one of the bad guys," Marlene said. "Sorry, Jack."

"I hate to say I told you so, man," Silas said, sounding half-drunk. "No, wait. I must've been thinking of somebody else. I *love* to say I told you so. And I did. Tell you so. But still, bummer about your girlfriend. Does anybody else feel the room rising?"

"It's the pain meds," Jack said. He turned back to Marlene. "Did they already disable her phone?"

She nodded. "Everything shut off before they even left the building. They could've gone anywhere."

"These guys are obviously dangerous," Jack said. "Do you think it's safe here for Silas?"

"I thought it was till you said that," Silas said. "Now I'm not gonna be able to sleep."

"Don't worry," Marlene said. "I'll stay."

"No offense," said Silas, "but I don't think you're a match for trained criminals."

Marlene shot Silas a look, then lifted her purse and dumped it onto the food tray of his bed. Scattered across the tray, intermingled with cosmetics and old receipts, were a can of pepper spray, a Taser, a butterfly knife, and a Bersa Thunder .380 handgun with an extra clip.

"Never mind, Jack," said Silas. "I think we're good here."

39

Jack spent the night tearing apart his condo, looking for some kind of evidence that Fleming might have left behind. As far as he could tell, she left virtually no trace of herself anywhere. He even took apart his land-line phone to check for bugs, even though he wasn't sure exactly what he was looking for.

He was so absorbed in his search for clues that, until he turned on the early morning news, he had completely forgotten what day it was:

Election day.

He had to vote; as an elector, it was unthinkable to not vote, even though it was clear that Randell would carry the state with or without his help. His polling place was back in Nobles, which meant leaving the dangerous world of political conspiracy behind for a few hours so he could perform his civic duty.

Maybe he could see Vera Lynn while he was there. He hadn't talked to her since the fight about Dad. Now that he felt he could be in danger, he didn't want to risk the possibility that they might never get a chance to patch things up.

As he walked to his car, he was accosted by a red-cheeked young pollster with a clipboard. "Hello sir. Did you know that only seven percent of eligible voters participated in the last city council election?"

Jack didn't slow down. "That's all, huh?"

"I know, right? Who on earth would willingly put their fate in the hands of such a small number of people they don't even know?"

"Good question," Jack said, and kept walking.

"Remember to vote!" the pollster yelled after him.

When he got to Nobles, he stopped by the house first, but it was dark and empty. She usually helped out as an election inspector, which meant being gone from early in the morning until well after the polls closed. He went to the polling station, figuring he would find her there.

"Jack," Dottie Jenkins said with some panic in her voice, "have you seen Vera Lynn?"

"I thought she was here," he said.

"She's supposed to be. It's not at all like her to just not show up."

A feeling of dread crept over Jack. Of course they would go after the people close to him. He was ashamed that he hadn't thought to warn Vera Lynn the night before.

He got the voting out of the way and went back to the house. There was no sign of a struggle anywhere; even the precariously arranged pig knickknacks on the porch rail were undisturbed. He drove around town, stopping at every house he knew to ask if anyone had seen her. He checked at the diner, the grocery store, all three gas stations, and the library. No one had seen her at all since the day before.

It was late in the afternoon—after he had ruled out every possible location he could think of—when Jack's phone finally rang. The display showed the caller: "Fleming."

He picked up, but said nothing.

"Hey Jack," she said. "Miss me?"

"Where is she?" he asked.

"Last time might have been fun and games, but this time it's real. If you want to see your sister alive again, you're going to have to do what we say."

"Fine. But let me talk to her."

"I don't think so. In fact, I think it's time to hang up. You never know who might be listening in."

The call dropped.

Regardless of what Fleming had said before about talking to the police, Jack came to the realization that he could not find Vera Lynn on his own. He drove to the Nobles County Sheriff's Office and marched straight into Sheriff Sempel's office.

"Sheriff, they've got my sister," he said.

"What's that supposed to mean?" Sempel asked.

"Vera Lynn. She's been kidnapped."

"And how do you know this?"

"They called me and told me."

"Who's this 'they' you're talking about?"

"I don't know exactly. But they're trying to steal the presidential election."

"Steal the election," Sempel repeated.

"Yes."

"In Texas."

"I know it sounds crazy. I just... I need help."

Sempel sat back and scratched his stomach. "I can check with her friends, start a clock ticking. If she hasn't turned up in a couple days-"

"I've already talked to her friends. She's not at home, nobody's seen her anywhere since yesterday. She never made it to the polling station today to help out. Have you ever known my sister to miss something like that?"

"Maybe she ran off with a male friend," Sempel said.

"She didn't run off with anybody. She was taken."

"I appreciate your anxiety, but that ain't cause to go round up a search party. We got certain procedures to follow."

"You're just Mister By-the-Book, huh? When did that happen? After you blackmailed my dad to help you get elected?"

Sempel pushed his chair back from his desk. "You don't wanna still be in here when I stand up," he said.

Jack stomped out of the office and out of the station. He saw Waylon sitting on a bench outside in his court clothes, smoking. Jack tried to speed up, but as soon as Waylon spotted him, he whistled and waved him over.

"Waylon, I'm sorry but I don't have time right now," Jack said, and kept walking.

Waylon sprang off the bench and jogged up to Jack. "Hold up," he said, and Jack finally stopped.

Jack realized that he hadn't seen Waylon since the convention incident. For all he knew, Waylon might be gearing up to punch him in the face. "Look, I'm sorry about the credentials challenge," Jack said, keeping his hands hovering around chest-level in case he needed to shield his head from a rain of blows.

Waylon waved him off as he took a drag on his cigarette. "Hil should've told me the parole thing was a problem. I guess he just figured nobody would say nothing, with him being sheriff."

"I'm sure he was just trying to look out for you," Jack said.

Waylon took one last drag and flicked his cigarette butt out into the street. "Hil's determined to make me a stand-up member of the community," he said, "whether I want to be or not. That's why he's got me working up here at the station. Just clerking, nothing I could cause much harm with. But it keeps the PO off my back."

"Glad to hear everything's going well," Jack said, inching toward his car door. "But seriously, I've got something I have to deal with right now-"

"So something really happened to Vera Lynn, huh?"

Jack stopped. "How did you know?"

Waylon nodded back toward the police station. "Hil likes to keep his office window open after everybody else leaves. Also, you were kinda loud."

"Yeah, well, my sister's been kidnapped, so you'll have to excuse the volume."

"Hil didn't believe you, huh?"

Jack shook his head. "Or maybe he did and he just doesn't care. Either way, I'm on my own." He opened his car door.

"Was that true, what you said?" asked Waylon. "About Hil blackmailing your dad?"

Jack reluctantly nodded.

"Listen," Waylon said, glancing nervously back at the station. "I don't know about this election stuff, but if your sister needs help, I'd like to help her. She's always been kinder than most around here."

"I appreciate it," Jack said. "But I don't really know where to start."

"You know the Avery place, about five miles outside of town?"

"County Road 104, right?"

"Yeah," Waylon said. "Isabel Avery called the station earlier about somebody squatting in the barn behind her property. Says there's been lights on and a couple cars parked out next to it. That land's owned by Mister Higgs, and he's been in the nursing home for about a year, so she knows they don't belong there, whoever it is. She's worried they're gonna start a fire or something. Now maybe it's nothing. Or... maybe it's something."

"Did your brother check it out?"

"Nah. Bertie Avery campaigned against him the first time he ran for sheriff, so Hil wouldn't so much as piss in either of their mouths if they was dying of thirst. You may not have picked up on this yet, but my brother can hold a grudge."

40

By the time they got out to County Road 104, the sun was setting. They pulled off the road and parked in the overgrown culvert just past Isabel's house, then hopped the barb-wire fence into her pasture. It was rocky and full of cactus, and most of the other vegetation had burned up in the summer sun months ago, which meant the walk would be easy—but it also meant they wouldn't have much cover when they got close.

Mr. Higgs's barn was ancient and gray, sagging under the weight of its years, and yet still sturdier than any of his neighbors' newer barns. Whenever a blue norther hit, like a relentless freight train carrying a payload of winter down across the plains, that barn knew enough to give a little and let it pass; the newer barns just stood still and adamant, fighting the weather with all their might until they had nothing left and flew apart into pieces.

Jack and Waylon came up on it from the back side. One of the doors on the front was open, and they could see light spilling out onto the overgrown path before it. Two black sedans glinted in the light, and although Jack couldn't tell which, he knew one of them must be Fleming's.

They heard voices from inside. After a moment Jack realized that they were coming from a television or radio. He got close enough to peek through a crack between boards, and saw Vera Lynn in a chair near the back of the barn, closest to them. Her wrists were bound by what looked like heavy-duty zip ties.

Seated next to her was the large blond man, busying himself with his smartphone. The one with long hair—Miles, according to the call they'd intercepted before—held a portable TV in his lap; he continually shifted and messed with dials, trying to get a clear signal. Fleming leaned against the wall near the open door, talking to Mr. Buzz-Cut.

"You can't just eat a burger?" Mr. Buzz-Cut asked.

"You're already going into town anyway," Fleming said. "What does it matter if you stop at one place or two places?"

He just shook his head and headed out of the barn.

"Hey," Fleming said. "Don't forget your hat."

Mr. Buzz-Cut trudged back through the barn to a large green canvas bag, pulled out a ball cap, and then headed back out the door.

"It helps if you put it on your head," Fleming called after him as he left.

Jack heard one of the sedans start up, and they both dove to the ground. Its headlights made an arc just to the side of them as it pivoted and headed off toward town.

Waylon motioned toward an outbuilding over the fence and across the pasture they came from, and they silently moved away from the barn. When they got to the outbuilding—some kind of forgotten workshop for Mr. Avery no doubt, with everything coated in dust and cobwebs—Jack figured it was safe to talk.

"We should call your brother," Jack said. "Tell him we found her and let the police handle it."

"No," Waylon said, and even in the darkness, Jack could see a fierceness in his eyes. "I'm done counting on my brother to take care of things."

"But there's no way we can get her ourselves," Jack said. "There's four of them-"

"Three," Waylon corrected. "That other guy went out to get food." Waylon clicked on a small UV keychain light and began rummaging through the clutter inside the shed.

"Still. What's the plan? Do you have guns back at your place we could use?"

"Why do you assume I have guns? Because I have tattoos and I was in jail?"

"I just assume everybody out here has guns," Jack said.

"Not me," he said. "That'd violate my probation."

Jack was secretly relieved, since guns would take the scenario to a level he was afraid he wasn't cut out for. And as much as Waylon was unwilling to call his brother in for help, Jack was equally unwilling to leave now that he knew where Vera Lynn was.

Waylon shined his UV light on the wall near Jack. "Look out," he said, and Jack saw a bark scorpion glowing bright green in the hazy blue light. He backed away, stumbling over the handle of a shovel as he went.

Jack had been stung exactly once by a scorpion. When he was thirteen, he made the mistake of shoving his hand into a pile of dirty clothes on his bedroom floor, and that's where it had been hiding. The sting was bad enough, but the worst part was that every few seconds it felt like he was being stung again. Half an hour of that was enough to teach him to be more careful where he stuck his hands.

"Hey," said Waylon, "I got an idea." He picked up a discarded plastic drink cup and scooped the scorpion into it, covering the top with a scrap of cardboard. He searched in the crevices of the shed and under rotting pieces of wood outside, and ended up finding three more scorpions. Then he lifted a felled branch, and Jack heard him whisper, "Oh hell yeah."

Under the branch was a redheaded giant centipede, at least six inches long and not in the mood to be hassled. Its coloring was hard to see in the UV light, but Jack had seen them many times as a kid, and they were the stuff of nightmares: red-colored head, shiny black body, sickly yellow legs. They looked like they belonged in a rainforest in some untamed tropical nation far, far away.

Waylon maneuvered the centipede into his cup; fortunately the sides were too slick for the scorpions to climb out as he did so.

"So what's your plan?" Jack asked. "Throw bugs on them?"

"That blond guy is the one to worry about," Waylon said. "You spend as much time in prison as I did, you learn to spot the ones that are trouble. I'll climb up to the hayloft from the back side-"

226

"You sure you can do that?"

"You seen me climb before," Waylon said, and Jack had to admit that his dexterity was impressive. "Besides, we used to hang out up there and drink back in the day. Old Man Riggs never had no clue."

"So what do I do?" Jack asked.

"You make some kind of noise out front, throw a rock or something. When that girl goes outside to check, I'll drop a load of critters down on top of Blondie. You sneak in through the back door and get Vera Lynn free."

"The back door looked like it was padlocked," Jack said, remembering the layout from earlier.

"It is... but the wood around the hinges is so old and worn down you can just wiggle the screws out and pull the whole door off."

"I don't have anything to cut Vera Lynn loose," Jack said, looking around the shed.

"Here," said Waylon, and handed him a penknife from his pocket.

Jack took a deep breath. "So no police, huh?" he asked, hoping that Waylon would reconsider.

Waylon shook his head. "You don't want them anyway. They'll get in there and start shooting, and you think those kidnappers are gonna let Vera Lynn live if they get pinned down?"

They worked out the details and then silently headed back toward the barn. Waylon found his climbing spot—a series of boards nailed to the outside of the back wall, one every few feet up the side—and took the rim of the bug cup between his teeth, holding the cardboard lid in place with his upper lip, so he could climb with both hands.

Once he disappeared into the loft bay, Jack found the back door and started slowly, quietly working on the hinge screws. The whole time, Miles complained about the poor TV reception and lack of channels.

"I don't get why we can't just take her back to the Nexus," he said. "Are we just gonna camp out here for a month?"

"If that's what he tells you to do," the blond man said, "you do it."

Just as Waylon had said, the worn wood gave up the screws without a fight. Jack peeked through the crack between door and frame; there was enough old farm equipment piled at the back of the barn that Jack thought they might not even notice the door coming off. Once the hinge was free, he gently propped the door in place so he could create a distraction out front.

He found a few decent-sized rocks and hurled them into the open area in front of the barn, just outside the reach of light. But the sound of the television kept Fleming from picking up the dull thuds of the rocks. Jack eyed the sedan. Maybe he could bounce a rock under the car, create some noise from hitting the undercarriage or a tire rim. He hefted a good one, nearly the size of a tennis ball, and threw it hard. But the rock took a bad bounce, and instead of going under the car, he hit the driver's side door dead on with a thunderous thump.

"What the hell?" Fleming said.

The long-haired guy turned down the television, eyes wide. "Please tell me there aren't chainsaw-wielding redneck psychos out here who want to wear our skin as a dress," he said.

When Jack saw Fleming move outside, he scrambled toward the back door and waited for Waylon to do his part. The noise had put the blond man on alert; he stood and moved in front of Vera Lynn. Jack waited patiently, holding the door steady, but his arm muscles were starting to quiver and burn; Waylon must have had to change position to track with the blond man, and the whole thing was taking longer than expected.

Just when Jack thought he might have to let go of the door, he saw a stream of dark silhouettes drop onto the blond man. One of the scorpions landed on his head, and another bounced off his back and hit the ground... but two scorpions and the centipede went straight down the back of his shirt and disappeared.

He shouted something that sounded like "Ha!" and struggled to scratch at his back. He kept yelling and danced around the barn floor, kicking up dust clouds, struggling to untuck his shirt and pull it off. The long-haired guy just sat there, trying to make sense of what he was seeing.

Jack moved the door aside and stepped carefully through the farm equipment. He stayed low and in the shadows as he snuck up behind Vera Lynn. "Hey," he whispered, and as she turned her head, he said, "Don't look back. Just act natural."

The blond man had his shirt off by then, but the critters were apparently still in his undershirt. The long-haired guy had joined in, trying to help pull off the undershirt as he shouted, "What's happening? What's happening?"

Jack sliced through the zip ties on Vera Lynn's ankles and wrists. As she yanked the duct tape from her mouth and turned to look into Jack's eyes, he heard someone shout "Stop!"

The blond man was naked from the waist up, but aside

from the errant twitch, he had recovered his senses. He lurched toward them, and the next thing Jack saw was a dark figure flying through the air, leaping down from the hayloft and tackling the blond man.

Jack pulled Vera Lynn toward the back of the barn, toward freedom and the cover of darkness. A gunshot rang out and Jack stopped dead; it had come so close to his head that he felt the air split next to his ear.

Fleming was back inside the barn. She trained the gun on Jack, but it was enough to stop Waylon cold too.

"Hey," Miles said, "I thought the rule was no guns."

"Those rules are for you," Fleming said, "not me."

"Vera Lynn, this is Fleming, the girl I told you about," Jack said. "Turns out I may have oversold her a bit."

Fleming pulled out her phone and tapped the screen. A few seconds later, she said, "It's me. We've got him here, with one other guy. Am I clear?" Pause. "Not a problem." She hung up and tucked her phone in her jacket.

"That's a relief," Fleming said, genuinely unburdened. "See, I've been having a hell of a time coming up with ways to kill people and make it look like an accident so nobody gets suspicious. But out here, I've got space... I've got time... and most importantly, I've got permission to make all three of you disappear completely. Which means it doesn't matter how I kill you."

"You got any idea who my brother is?" said Waylon.

"Shut up, Jethro," Fleming said. She turned back to Jack. "I know this isn't how you imagined things working out between us, Jack. But I just want you to know that the time we spent together was so very..." She searched the air for the word. "Boring."

Fleming held the gun with both hands to steady her aim at Jack's head. He pushed Vera Lynn off to the side, but held her hand tight. He kept his eyes open. He was determined to meet his fate head on.

But instead Jack saw Fleming's head cock forward and to the side, and a split second later the sound of a distant rifle shot caught up. She crumpled and fell.

Unsure of where the shot came from, the other two kidnappers stayed low and ran for their car. They got in and tore off down the dirt road, leaving Jack, Vera Lynn, and Waylon behind.

Waylon crawled over to the other two, keeping one arm tight to his body. "Everybody okay?" he asked.

Jack and Vera Lynn were still in a huddled daze when a figure, dressed all in black, stepped into the light of the barn. The figure carried a high-powered rifle in one hand, and a briefcase in the other.

"Hold on," Jack said. "She's one of them."

Candace lowered the rifle. "Not anymore," she said.

41

"I've been watching them since last night," Candace said. "I tried to get the police out here to take care of it on their own so you wouldn't be involved. I called the station pretending to be a neighbor, said I saw some suspicious activity, but nobody ever came out."

"You picked the wrong neighbor to be," Waylon said.

"Do you think they're coming back?" asked Jack.

Candace shook her head. "Maybe for her if they get the chance"—she glanced over at Fleming's body—"but not for you. They'll regroup. Try to come at you some other way." She opened the briefcase, which contained foam padding cut to fit around the rifle's component parts. With a rag, she unscrewed the muzzle brake from the end of the barrel and fit it into the case.

"Then we need to expose them," Jack said. "Before somebody gets hurt." Out of the corner of his eye, he could see just enough of Fleming's lifeless body to know that he didn't want to look any closer. "Before somebody *else* gets hurt."

"You can't," Candace said. She slid the rifle bolt out, tucked it away, and started unscrewing the barrel. "They'll boot you as an elector, so you'll lose whatever leverage you have. Plus, no one will believe you until after the votes are cast. Then they'll wonder how exactly you knew what was going on, and why you didn't stop it. Trust me… by the time they're through, you'll be the villain of the story."

"Why should I trust you?" asked Jack. "You were the one offering me a million bucks to change my vote."

"You shouldn't trust me," she said. "Or anyone else." She laid the barrel carefully in the case and pressed it into place. "But I did just save your life, so there's that."

For a fleeting moment Jack thought about thanking her, but it all seemed too strange. There must be some ulterior motive behind it. "Why the change of heart?" he asked. "You seemed pretty gung-ho for the other guys before."

The question was clearly one that she herself had spent a great deal of time considering. "I used to think it was okay to do bad things if you had good reasons," she said. "But now…" She slapped the butt of the rifle and it telescoped into the rest of the stock, neat and compact. "All we are is what we do. Everything else is just excuses." She folded the rifle's bipod legs in against the body and tucked the last piece away in the case.

"They're going to keep coming after me," Jack said. "You said so. Can you help me stop them?"

"I did what I needed to do. Time for me to disappear. Your friends should disappear too, if they want to stay safe."

"I'm not running from these bastards," Vera Lynn said.

"Please," said Jack. "I can't put you in danger like that again."

"We got a hunting cabin out west," Waylon said. "I can take Vera Lynn out there until this is all over. If it pleases her."

Vera Lynn thought it over, then nodded reluctantly. "Thank you, Waylon. That'd be all right."

Jack reached out and touched Candace's shoulder. She flinched, but did not move away. "I know you know these guys," Jack said. "Tell me how I can beat them."

"Don't try to go through them," she said. "They're fighters... you're not. Find a way around them." She picked up the gun case. "You're a good guy, Jack. Do what you are, and I'm sure you'll figure something out." Before he could say anything else, she turned and strode out into the darkness.

*   *   *

Waylon's trailer was an older single-wide dropped square in the middle of a grubby acre just outside of town. There were three cars out front, but only one—a compact Korean hatchback—was fully assembled.

"Just go straight to the cabin, okay?" Jack told Vera Lynn. "Don't go by the house for clothes or anything... they could be waiting there."

Waylon nodded. "Don't worry. I'll keep her safe."

Vera Lynn held Jack's head between her hands. "You just look out for yourself, hear me?" She kissed his forehead, then hugged him hard.

After Jack left, Waylon filled a banana box with some canned foods, drinks, and a wad of clothing. "You can wear some of my stuff if it doesn't bother you," he said.

They loaded up the hatchback and headed out onto the highway. "Wait a second," Vera Lynn said. "I thought the cabin was west."

"It is," said Waylon. "And I'm taking you there, and I'll make sure nobody comes within half a mile of you. But first we're gonna see my brother."

"Jack doesn't want the law involved," she said. "If they find out, they won't let him be an elector."

"We won't even say Jack's name. Just tell Hil what happened when they took you and maybe he can catch these sons of bitches."

When they got to Hil's house, he was already in his underwear and a bathrobe, ready for bed. They told him the story of Vera Lynn's kidnapping, subtracting out Jack when they described the rescue.

When they finished, Hil sat back in his chair and sighed heavily. "Why in the hell didn't you just call me?" he asked. Waylon had no answer he was willing to give.

"There's got to be a way to catch 'em," said Waylon. "Maybe we could use that sketch artist program you got down the station."

"Sketches don't catch nobody," Hil said. "You need a photo, and even then, who knows where they went. Ain't much I can do."

"Listen to me, brother," said Waylon. "I heard you and Jack talking earlier at the station. I know why you been trying to do all these things for me. Well, I'm done relying on you. But this... at the very least, you owe me this."

Hil looked hurt. It was an emotion precious few had ever

seen him wear on the outside.

Finally Vera Lynn broke the silence. "One of them," she said, "the guy with the buzz-cut. He went up to the Whataburger and the Subway around about seven to pick up dinner. You might could find him on their security tapes."

Hil rubbed his eyes and face, resigning himself to a late night. "All right. Lemme call the owners."

42

M̲ILES AND V̲IG met up with Platt at a motel on the outskirts of South Austin. They had debated going back for Fleming's body, but Langhorne decided it wasn't worth the risk. "There's no way they can identify her anyway," Langhorne told them.

Vig switched out the license plates on the two cars, just in case anyone had gotten a glimpse of them. He kept a stack of four or five plates in the trunk of each car, hidden down where the spare tire sat.

The three ate their dinner late and cold, sitting on the edge of a lopsided bed, passing around the paper sacks that Platt was out fetching when the whole operation went to hell. "If I'd been there," he said, "no way they'd of gotten away."

"Whatever," Miles muttered.

"What'd you say?" Platt threw his limp half-burger on the floor and stood.

"Quiet," Vig told them, and pointed at the TV.

News coverage of the election was in full swing, though most of the discussion barely even qualified as preliminary. Two different stations were hinting that Randell would take every last one of the swing states in the East, which matched Langhorne's analysis from so many months before.

"The one bright spot for the president in today's election," the newscaster said, "is Nevada. Exit polls and early returns show the president leading against Governor Randell by a small but consistent margin, which defies the predictions of most of the pundits we've talked to.

"The same cannot be said for the Midwest, where the president has lost significant support in recent months due to the troubled economy. That loss of support in Ohio and Indiana and Minnesota in particular just might have—and I'm only speculating at this point—just might have sealed his fate as a one-term president."

"We got Nevada?" said Miles.

"That puts us at... 256 to 282," Platt said, "even if we lose the other swings."

"Twenty-six point spread," Miles said. "Fourteen electors is all we need. We got that, easy."

Platt and Miles, on the verge of a fistfight moments before, high-fived each other. "Hey, watch the fries," Vig said as the bed shifted, but even the stone-faced Scandinavian—with his back still swollen from scorpion stings and centipede bites—couldn't help but crack a smile at the news.

*   *   *

"Sir, I think you'll want to see this," Grant said.

Langhorne had just woken up to confirmed reports that Randell had won the election by the slimmest electoral margin since 2000, 282 to 256. The news about the president's victory in Nevada, barely a passing mention in most election coverage since Randell won anyway, put Langhorne in high spirits.

But the look on Grant's face was not one of celebration. He handed a sheet of paper to Langhorne. It was a BOLO from the Nobles County Sheriff's Office for a suspect wanted in connection to a kidnapping. In the middle of the page were two images from security cameras, apparently taken at fast-food restaurants. The man in the images was clearly visible and was, quite unmistakably, Vincent Platt. Contrary to orders, he was not wearing a ball cap.

Langhorne calmly pulled out his phone and dialed. When Vig answered, he said, "Do not come back to the Nexus. Plans have changed."

*   *   *

As they entered Austin city limits, Vig—seated alone in the back of the sedan—told Miles to keep driving. They had abandoned the car with a damaged door in a shopping center parking lot, just in case, and were all three riding together.

"We make one stop first," he said, consulting a GPS application on his phone.

Vig directed Miles to stay on Highway 71, which skimmed the southern part of the city and passed the airport before quickly returning to rural isolation.

Platt turned and looked back from the passenger seat.

"Where we headed?" he asked.

Vig said nothing, and continued staring at his phone.

"We're all on the same team, you know," Platt said, and turned back around. "It wouldn't hurt to share information."

After a minute or so, Vig turned off his phone and reached into his waist pack. "Watch for the next interchange," he said. "Go north." Platt was busy watching for road signs when Vig slipped the industrial zip tie over his head and pulled it taut, crushing Platt's windpipe back against the headrest of his seat.

Platt flailed his arms wildly, and Miles nearly lost control of the car before Vig grabbed Platt's hands and pulled them behind his seat, cuffing them together with another zip tie.

"What the hell!" Miles screamed and slammed on the brakes.

"Keep driving," Vig said, in a tone so ominous that Miles immediately shut up and stepped on the gas.

Platt quickly lost consciousness, his head lolling toward the side window. He looked like he was napping.

Miles turned the car onto the northbound highway as instructed. The pavement rose and the ground dropped out below, leaving them on an elevated stretch.

"Stop after these trees," Vig said.

Miles pulled the car toward the narrow shoulder, edged only by a low concrete median. Once they passed the trees, the deep green water of the Lower Colorado River was visible thirty feet below.

Vig deftly snipped the zip ties on Platt's neck and hands, giving his head a quick snap just to make sure the job was done. He checked to make sure no other vehicles were approaching, then got out and opened the front passenger door.

With one swift gesture, he flung Platt's body out and over the concrete barrier. At the sound of the splash, Miles flinched as if a gun had been fired next to his ear.

Vig got back in, this time in Platt's now-vacant seat. "Okay," he said with a nod. "Now we go to the Nexus."

.

43

Jack sat in the dank storm cellar of the family house in No-bles, his father's Winchester pump-action shotgun laid across his lap as he worked. After leaving Vera Lynn and Waylon, he had spent the night gathering supplies. He didn't dare go back to his condo. First he made a trip to the office, where he picked up his computer, scanner, favorite printer, laminator, and assorted print media. Next was a trip to the always-open Walmart for food and ammunition.

Finally, he settled in for the long haul at a place he knew well—the very place he told Vera Lynn to avoid. There was only one entrance to the storm cellar, and he situated himself with his back to the wall, facing it. If they were going to come for him, he would be ready.

In the meantime, he was determined to figure out a way to stop their plan. Candace had said "Do what you are," so he brought his work gear just in case he thought of a way to make his seemingly irrelevant graphic design skills pay off.

But first, he had to learn everything he could about their plan. How did they do it? Who was involved? What were the weaknesses? He lost track of the days chasing lead after lead across the Internet, eating meals out of cans and bags, sleeping only in short bursts, always waking up in a panic, unsure if the noise he heard was real or just the lingering remnant of a dream.

He checked in with Vera Lynn and Marlene often, just to make sure no one had come after them again. They were safe; Vera Lynn spent her days reading *Lonesome Dove* aloud to Waylon, since Hil had left a tattered paperback copy of the book in the cabin during the previous hunting season. Silas was out of the hospital, and Marlene was temporarily staying with him to serve as both nurse and protector.

Jack went through every Republican Party rule book and every legislative procedure he could find. He recreated his brief conversations with Candace in his mind, trying to uncover the smallest pieces of information that might guide him. For example, she had said the electors would get to vote privately. How did they get a law like that passed? Did they have someone working on the inside? If so, how could Jack hope to bypass them?

After all his research, he came back to a single offhand comment that Silas had made months before. That, he concluded, was the key to beating them at their game.

He would need a special staff badge for access at the Capitol; his elector badge would only get him to the floor and gallery of the chamber, and there would be tight security on the first day of the new session. It took some research and experimenting, but after a few tries Jack came up with a badge that looked practically indistinguishable from the real thing.

He also needed a suit. Since all his clothes were back in Austin, he risked the short trip upstairs to his dad's old bedroom. It was almost just as he had last seen it, except the bed was empty and neatly made. The place on the dresser where the pen box had sat was still less dusty than the area around it. The picture of him, his dad, and President Reagan still hung in the same spot on the wall. Jack wanted it for himself, for his own wall, but did not want to disturb the sanctity of the room. Besides, he needed to make sure he was going to live through this first.

Ray Patton was a good deal larger than Jack for most of his life, but he never got rid of any of his old clothes. Jack went deep into the closet and found a navy suit that looked about right, or at least not comically large. He pulled it out and tried it on; it wasn't perfect, and was a bit outdated, but it was close enough. As he looked in the mirror, he caught glimpse of the Reagan picture again.

He was wearing the exact suit his father had worn on that day in 1981.

44

THE RANDELL SCANDAL was playing perfectly. It had picked up the name "Arms for Abdul" somewhere along the way, and fresh revelations were dominating every news cycle. They had managed to eke out a few soundbites from notable Republican leaders conceding that, if it were true, the scandal could have "dire consequences" for Randell's presidency. Even if the whole glorious concoction evaporated in the sunlight of scrutiny a week from now, it was still enough to open the door for the justification of faithless electors.

"Still no sign of Patton at his condo," Miles reported to Langhorne. "And his office hasn't been open for a couple weeks at least."

"Forget about him for now," said Langhorne, busily scribbling on a whiteboard. "We have the votes without him. It's down to the four of us and we still have plenty to do. If Patton dares to turn up at the Capitol to try and cause a scene, you can take care of him then."

The next order of business was to arrange for paying off the faithless electors. They had been instructed to arrive in Austin two days before the vote so that initial payments could be made and voting details discussed. Nearly all of them followed these instructions and called the secured phone line with their hotel and room info. As Miles put together the list for payment delivery, he said, "Robeson hasn't checked in yet."

Miles tried calling Robeson's cell and his Sugar Land number, but got no answer at either.

"Leave it," Vig said. "We don't need him anymore."

"I'm gonna drive out there," said Miles. "This guy's already taken us for a million. We can't just let him blow us off, right?"

Vig sighed. "We make deliveries first."

The delivery route took them to seven different hotels, mostly downtown but two that were closer to the airport. None of the eighteen packages contained cash; the earlier displays of stacks of hundred-dollar bills were for visual impact, and for the ten thousand in earnest money they gave to each elector.

Instead, the packages each contained a statement from the First Royal Bank of Anguilla indicating the deposit amount (half a million, with the rest to follow after the vote), as well as a bank card in the name of a shell corporation set up specifically for the elector. They were given the option to name these shell companies themselves. Most of the electors went for mundane, believable names that would not arouse suspicion, such as Brandwell Financial Solutions Incorporated. One opted for Heart of Texness Imports. Another chose My Happy Ending Inc.

They made the deliveries out near the airport their last two stops, and from there continued east. Vig made Miles call Langhorne first to ask permission, since the drive to Sugar Land meant they wouldn't get back until well after dark. Miles, the driving force behind the trip, ended up sleeping through most of it. When they finally arrived, Nolan Robeson's estate looked the same from the outside, except for the Notice of Sale posted on the front door.

The door was locked, but Vig knocked out the large leaded glass insert in the center and they stepped through. Inside, the house was almost empty. The kitchen cabinets were gone, as was the chef-grade gas range and custom hand-hammered copper hood that had once sat above it. In the living room, there was only a single leather recliner and a large flat-screen TV.

Nolan Robeson was in the recliner, yellow and stiff. His body was surrounded by empty booze bottles and ruptured foil blister packs.

Miles dry-heaved and looked away. "Oh God... he's dead, isn't he?"

"Yes," said Vig. "Probably only two, three days. Not too smelly yet." He bent down and scooped up some of the empty blister packs. "Hydrocodone. Oxycodone. Methylphenidate. Some of everything."

Vig scattered the packs on the floor and headed to leave. "This is why you don't give all the money up front," he said.

"This was my idea," said Miles. "What's Langhorne going to do? Do you think..." He couldn't finish, but the look of dread on his face was clearer than words.

"Come on," Vig said. "You worry later."

45

THE CAPITOL was abuzz with activity for the first day of session. Security was as tight as Jack had expected. He kept the access badge marked "Elector" in his pocket, and instead clipped on the one marked "Staff." Instead of waiting in the longer line, which had a walk-through metal detector, Jack walked confidently to a shorter line where an officer waved a wand over his limbs and torso, and sent him through.

Once he got past the south lobby and rotunda, the crowd thinned considerably. That was when he spotted Vig, the tall blond man from the barn. He was wearing a suit and access badge, just like Jack. Before Jack could even move to hide, Vig noticed him and started walking in his direction.

Jack headed toward the rear of the building as fast as he could without calling attention to himself. He exited into the hazy morning gray and headed north, past the street-level skylights of the underground Capitol Extension. He could go back down into the underground Extension, where the maze of offices might allow him to remain hidden, or continue north to the half-empty parking lots on Congress Avenue, possibly closer to safety but farther away from the Capitol and his mission.

Jack opted to head underground, and walked swiftly toward one of the two elevator pavilions that flanked the open-air rotunda at the center of the extension complex. As he approached, a man came out of one of the pavilions. He had his phone to his ear and was facing away at first. *Just a staffer*, he told himself, and kept moving forward.

But when the man turned around, he could see it was Miles, the long-haired one from the barn. Jack bolted toward the elevator on the opposite side of the rotunda, but Vig had caught up and cut him off. The two men closed in, pinning Jack to the rail that lined the rotunda.

He knew they wouldn't kill him here. But if they took him somewhere, out of public view, that would be it. He couldn't let them take him away. He backed up against the rail, gripping it tightly.

With nowhere else to go, he looked over the rail to the open-air rotunda. It made him dizzy, lightheaded. *It's not the height*, he remembered telling Waylon, *it's the prospect of falling*. The distance to the bottom was too great to land safely, but part of the way down—thirty feet?—a walkway ringed the structure. If he hung onto the bottom of the rail, that would probably make it more like a twenty-five foot drop. He turned to see Vig and Miles drawing closer. He took a deep breath and hopped the rail.

It took more strength than he expected to hold his weight,

and for a moment he was sure he'd slip off. But he held fast, and as the two men rushed toward the edge where he went over, Jack worked his hands downward to the bottom of the rail.

"Grab him!" shouted Vig.

Jack looked down between his dangling feet. The walkway seemed so much farther away than it had before. He hesitated, and before he could let go, he felt two hands grab him by his jacket sleeves. Two more meaty hands groped over the top of the rail, trying to haul him in like a gaffed amberjack.

In a panic, Jack let go. He dropped only a few inches, his hands hung up by his jacket cuffs, which were in the tight grip of one of the men. But Jack could feel that the man's hands were slipping against all his weight. Just as Vig snagged the collar of Jack's coat, Jack slipped free and plummeted, leaving his empty jacket behind.

The impact sent a blinding bolt of pain from his right heel all the way up to his brain. He crumpled as he landed, banging his chin against his knee and rolling onto his back, writhing in agony. Staring up at the sky, he could see the two men peering over the rail.

"Elevator," Vig said, and they disappeared.

Jack knew he had to stand up and get moving. He was certain he'd broken something in his foot, but he couldn't worry about that yet. He rolled over to his knees and struggled to pull himself upright. He limped through a door that led south, back toward the Capitol, and found himself between a bank of four committee rooms, empty and dark. He went into the closest one, and as he did, the motion-sensing lights clicked on.

The lights would be a dead giveaway that someone was in the room. He went back out to the hall and tried to think of something else. That was when he noticed the drops of blood that betrayed his route. He look at his hand; the outer edge was red and slick.

He knew it wouldn't take long for the two men to get downstairs, and there was no way he could outrun them. The blood trail would lead them straight to him. He looked at the other open rooms, all dark. An idea struck him.

If he couldn't move fast enough to get away, maybe he could move slowly enough.

He hobbled a ways down the hall, toward the tunnel that led back to the Capitol, making sure that blood dripped from his hand the whole way. When he reached an intersection with a hallway leading to staff offices, he covered his hand and doubled back as quickly as he could with his injured foot.

He limped to one of the remaining dark committee rooms, and slowly shifted his body through the doorway. The motion was so slow that the sensor for the room lights could not detect him. He got all the way inside before he shifted suddenly on his bad foot and the light clicked on. He shuffled over to the third room to try again. He knew time was running out.

He entered the room slowly, so slowly that he was sure the two men would appear in the hall at any moment. He was careful not to rely on his injured foot, straining to maintain control over every muscle in his body. He kept his breathing as steady as possible to avoid expanding his chest too greatly. It was like a slow-motion ballet.

He kept his eyes glued to the hall until his head disappeared into the darkness of the room. He still wasn't hidden;

if someone else so much as peeked inside, they would spot him right away. He painstakingly moved toward an arcing row of chairs at the closest end of the room. The chairs lined a semicircular bench outfitted with microphones, a typical committee dais that faced outward to the rest of the room. If he could get under the bench without triggering the lights, he figured he would have a chance.

As he made his way there, slowly and painfully, he could hear the footfalls of the two men racing up the hall. He had to force himself to keep his movements slow and deliberate; every inch of his body was screaming at him to run.

Jack's heart leapt into his throat as he heard them race past the open committee room door. They kept going. He allowed himself a moment of relief, but continued toward the bench. He feared that they would be back.

Sure enough, after less than a minute, he could hear the men moving closer again. "You think he doubled back?" Miles asked.

"*I* would," said Vig. "Check these rooms."

He heard the men moving through the room next door— one of the two rooms where he had triggered the lights on. By the sound of it, they were upending tables and chairs, opening every cabinet and drawer. Checking every possible place to hide.

Jack made it to the bench and slowly crouched under it. He thought he might be out of the sensor's range, but he couldn't be sure, so he maintained his deliberate pace. The men had moved on to the other lit committee room, tearing it apart with even greater determination than the first.

Jack was almost completely under the bench now—only

his injured foot still extended out into view. He dragged it toward him, inch by painful inch.

It occurred to him that the men had stopped ransacking the other room, and had gone quiet. Just then he heard someone breathing heavily at the doorway. The man's shoe squeaked as he stepped inside.

Jack yanked his foot under the bench just as the lights clicked on. The pain was blinding, but he clenched his teeth together to keep from crying out.

The man was still in the doorway, breathing. Jack heard more footsteps approach. "Anything?" Vig asked.

"No," Miles said. "The lights were out when I walked up. Maybe he made it to the staff offices."

The two men walked away, but Jack didn't take a single breath until their steps, echoing through the empty hallway, faded to silence.

46

Jack had already memorized where he needed to go, but he had no way of knowing where Vig and Miles were. He moved cautiously toward the staff offices. Most were empty, their occupants already in the main building or on the lawn out front doing interviews.

He had to double back, and took the long way around instead of exposing himself to the high visibility of the open-air rotunda. His destination was the northeast wing of offices—the farthest from the Capitol. It was slow going with his injured foot, but he tried to walk as inconspicuously as possible. He did not want to attract the attention of the Capitol police; if they saw his condition and took him in for questioning, he stood no chance of getting where he needed before session began.

About halfway there, Vig appeared—fifty yards down the hall, standing between Jack and his destination. Jack cut over into another wing, hoping Vig didn't spot him, but he heard the skitter of shoes on the terrazzo floors and knew the man was on his way.

The first door on the left was a cleaning supply closet. Jack ducked in. In one of the back corners, close-set rows of pipe ran from floor to ceiling, forming a narrow place to hide. Jack squeezed through the pipes and waited.

Vig entered the supply closet quietly, checking over every square inch as he advanced toward Jack. Finally he spotted him. "There you are," Vig said, and reached through the pipes to grab him.

Jack tried to fight him off, but Vig was too strong. He grabbed Jack by the throat and squeezed. Jack clawed at his hands, but they did not relent. He couldn't breathe, but even worse, he felt the blood building in his head and his vision was starting to close in on the sides. Jack had almost given up when he remembered...

Something.

In his pocket.

He reached in and pulled out his father's pen. With one vicious thrust, he stabbed the pen so far into Vig's hand that it came out the other side and poked Jack in his own neck. Vig yelled and loosened his grip, which gave Jack just enough time and space to squeeze through the pipes and drag himself away.

Vig lunged after him, but with the pen stabbed through his hand, he couldn't fit it back through the close-set pipes. He was still working on it as Jack stumbled out into the hall, toward the office of the one person that might still be able to help him save the election.

"Mister Haycombe?"

Donnie Lee Haycombe sat at the center of a storm of staffers and paperwork, barking orders in every direction. One frazzled assistant paused long enough to tell Jack, "Representative Haycombe is not available right now. We're preparing for session."

"I'm... I'm one of the presidential electors," Jack said. He was getting lightheaded; his injuries were finally catching up with him.

Another staffer noticed his battered state and grabbed him by the arm. "I can show you where you need to go," she said.

"No!" Jack said, too loudly. The staffers went silent. "I need to speak to Mister Haycombe."

Haycombe stood. "Son, I'd be happy to talk with you after session." Noticing Jack's bloody hand, he said, "You look like you need some medical attention. Could we get that for him?"

"I'm fine," Jack said. "But I need to talk to you about the electoral votes. They're going to steal the election."

Haycombe tilted his head back, peered down his moustache at Jack. "Uh huh. Son, it sounds like you might have hit your head pretty good. Why don't we get a nurse to check you out?" He turned to his staffers and waved them into action. "Put him on the couch, elevate his feet."

"I'm not delusional," Jack said. "I know about the voter privacy bill, and the real reason they wanted you to push it through."

It took a few seconds for the words to sink in, but when they did, Haycombe's expression darkened. "Give us the room," he said, and his staffers swiftly and silently exited. "Now what about the voter privacy bill?"

"It was part of the plan. They sold it to you as a union-busting tactic, didn't they? But it was really meant to give electors a secret ballot, so nobody would know who went faithless."

Haycombe spread his massive hands across his desk. "Son, I think somebody's been having fun with you. This all sounds like a giant crock of horse shit."

"I know it does," Jack said. "And nobody's willing to try and stop it because they don't want to look like they're insane. And that's why you're the only one who can help."

"Because I don't mind looking insane?"

"Because you're the one with the most to lose."

Haycombe looked amused. "Now just how do you figure that?" he asked.

"If I'm telling the truth, and you have at least fourteen electors cast votes for the current president instead of Randell, nobody is going to know which electors betrayed the party. All of them will deny it. But then people are going to wonder, how on earth did this voter privacy bill get passed just in time to cover up for those faithless electors? Was it coincidence? Or was it part of the plan? Who was responsible for this bill? And I think we both know the answer there."

Haycombe shifted in his chair. "You think you and your friends can set me up, I will crucify you, have no doubt about that."

"I'm not a part of it. I'm trying to stop it."

"If... *if*... all this nonsense was true, it wouldn't matter anyway. Session is about to start. Even if I could get enough votes to repeal it, I can't get voter privacy back on the agenda this late."

"True," said Jack. "But there is still one thing you can do."

47

A STAFFER ESCORTED JACK to the bathroom to clean up, then to the chamber floor. The other electors were already there, waiting in a long line. Jack scanned the line of people, and found that he could not even begin to guess which ones were the faithless electors, just minutes away from betraying their party and helping to steal the election. They all looked normal. They all looked nervous.

Because the vote was to be by secret ballot, the electors were each given a clipboard that held a custom-made voting ballot listing the candidates for president and vice president. There was a small privacy booth arranged at the back of the gallery, and the electors were instructed to walk back to the booth to complete their ballot. They would then fold the ballot and place it in an accompanying envelope, which would be collected by the speaker and tallied for the six Certificates of Vote. The Certificates of Vote would then have to be signed by each elector, verifying the count.

The session opened with some short speeches from a handful of special guests, none of whom Jack recognized or bothered to pay attention to. All he could think about was whether or not Haycombe would follow through. Jack couldn't get a read on the man, and he wasn't sure Haycombe fully bought the threat, either. But he took his swing, and now it was just a matter of waiting to see where the ball landed.

After the speeches, the chair pulled out the Certificates of Ascertainment that listed the state's electors. The certificates were not yet verified or signed by the governor. Until they were, Jack and the other electors were not recognized as members of the electoral college. Once that happened, all hope of stopping the faithless electors was lost.

The speaker held the certificates as he spoke with one of Haycombe's staffers, then with some of his own people. It seemed to Jack like hours went by, watching the speaker hesitate, then move toward his podium with the certificates, then stop again for further consultation.

"I'd like to call a short recess," the speaker finally said. "We got some paperwork issues we need to straighten out." As the people in the gallery began chattering and milling around, he returned to the microphone. "Now would be the perfect time for our electors to gather on the front lawn for photos with their respective representatives."

The legislators and the electors filed out of the chamber, with just a handful of representatives remaining behind. The electors left their clipboards and ballots, still blank, on a long table by one of the entrances. Jack made no move to leave; he put his clipboard on the pile, but slipped the ballot into his pocket.

A page approached and tried to escort Jack out to the lawn. "I'm not going anywhere," Jack said.

The page turned nervously to Haycombe, who made some hand signals that the page appeared to understand. "Okay," the page said, "but we'll need you to clear the floor. You can go up to the gallery if you want."

Jack struggled up the stairs to the gallery on the second floor, using his arms to pull himself and keep the weight off his foot. The gallery was still dotted with spectators, though most had taken a break along with the representatives.

As soon as the representatives and their electors were busy posing for a phalanx of photographers outside, Haycombe's team of assistants quietly ushered in a few dozen people to stand along the wall where Jack had been. Then the staffers silently shut the chamber doors and secured them.

The speaker turned off his microphone and began talking quickly to the few legislators that remained inside. Jack couldn't make out most of what he said, which seemed to be the point. He did, however, hear the chair call for the submission of a new slate of electors. Haycombe offered up a list that he handed to the chair, who rapidly read through the names and called for a vote.

This was the essence of Jack's plan. He had remembered that state lawmakers possessed full control over how their state's electors were chosen. "They could have three old men go into a closet and spin a bottle if they wanted," Silas had told him.

And that's what had given him the idea. If the legislature replaced the entire slate of electors—including himself—with a brand-new batch of people pulled from the crowd gathered at the Capitol, then no one would have a chance to coerce them or buy their vote.

It required a certain amount of faith that the average voter would, when put in a position of power, do the right thing and cast their vote in accordance with the majority of the state. But after everything that he had been through, Jack decided he would rather put his country's fate in the hands of normal people than trust the pledges of Party cronies.

The new electors waited in a cluster on the ground floor. Some were employees at the Capitol; some were simply interested spectators. All seemed genuinely excited to participate in the affairs of government—the exact feeling that Jack had once hoped to experience, back before the whole beautiful illusion of the democratic process came crashing down around him.

The vote on the new slate of delegates was chaotic. The handful of legislators present in the chamber dashed around to all the empty desks, pressing the "Yea" voting buttons of all the absent representatives. At the same time, some of the people outside must have realized that the legislature was back in session, because Jack could hear pounding and yelling at the chamber doors as Haycombe's staff—backed up by the Capitol's team of police officers—held them closed. Haycombe must have convinced the police that there was an imminent security risk outside.

The other spectators in the gallery were confused and alarmed. "Do you think it's a bomb threat?" one woman whispered. "No, no, they're just voting," another said. "But then where's everybody else?" her friend asked. "They're doing something shady," said an old man. "You can tell by how they're all moving around."

When the vote board showed a majority of green lights, the chair carried the motion approving the new electors. New Certificates of Ascertainment were issued on the spot, and the electors each quickly completed their ballots.

Although the vote was meant to be secret, the first elector came out of the booth and called out, "I cast my vote for James Randell, the next President of the United States!"

Each subsequent elector followed suit, publicly proclaiming their support for Randell. In the end, all thirty-eight electors cast their votes for Republican nominee James Randell.

The new electors signed the six Certificates of Vote, passing the copies along in a line, and delivered them to the speaker. The governor quickly signed them, certifying the result. The small group of lawmakers, staff, and electors applauded as the governor signed the final document and held it up for all to see.

The celebrations inside the chamber were no match for the rising tide of commotion outside. With the votes certified and sealed, Haycombe's staff relented and the chamber was flooded with lawmakers and reporters. There would be countless questions, allegations, accusations, and investigations—sound and fury, signifying nothing. Jack could already hear some staffers proclaiming that the doors had been secured due to security issues, and that the problem had been resolved thanks to everyone's cooperation. In the end, everything would return to normal, because that was what those in charge wanted.

And in the meantime, Jack was one of only a handful of

people in the world who knew that all the grandstanding and mock outrage that filled the chamber was a small price to pay, because at least the will of the people had been preserved.

48

"CLEVER," a voice said, and Jack turned around. The man sitting two rows behind him in the gallery was nondescript, almost invisibly so. Middle-aged, silver-templed, perfectly groomed.

Jack knew right away that the man was in on the plot. Judging by his quiet confidence, he might even be the person in charge. "Who are you?" he asked.

"Call me Langhorne," the man said.

"Guess this kind of ruins your plan," Jack said.

"Yes, it does."

Jack couldn't run, but he was braced for a fight if necessary. He didn't know if the man might draw a weapon and try to kill him on the spot. With all the commotion below, it might even go unnoticed.

"What happens now?" Jack asked.

"The original electors will cry foul," Langhorne said. "Even the ones who were bought off. In all likelihood, they'll be paid off again, this time by their own party. The official story will probably be that there was some kind of mechanical issue with the chamber doors, or some unsubstantiated security risk. Some poor schmuck will get fired as a scapegoat, but he'll collect a secret pension for not making a fuss about it. Egos will be massaged, campaign coffers will swell, and soon enough, everyone will forget this ever happened."

"What happens to me?" Jack asked.

"Enjoy your life," Langhorne said. "Forget about us, and we'll forget about you. You are no longer our concern. Unless, of course, you give us reason to be concerned."

Down below, a fistfight broke out on the chamber floor. Representatives that didn't know about the conspiracy were claiming—rightfully so, Jack thought—that their votes had been stolen.

"What kind of a system is this," Jack said, "where the only way you can get the right thing done is by cheating?"

"Welcome to politics," Langhorne said.

Capitol police stepped in and broke up the fight, but cameras continued to flash as one of the representatives gushed blood from his head.

"How many faithless votes did you have?" asked Jack.

"Eighteen without a doubt. And after the Nevada win, that would've been more than enough."

"They would've found a way to throw them out," said Jack.

"Would they? The state can't do that. The vote would fall to the House, and buying votes in the House is like driving an ice cream truck up K Street. Also, if my experience in Washington has taught me one thing, it's this: as hard as it might be to get anything done, it's ten times harder to get it undone."

"If my experience in Texas has taught me one thing," Jack said, "it's this: don't underestimate a pissed-off Republican."

"Enjoy your moment," said Langhorne. "In three more election cycles, Texas is going to turn Democrat without any help from me."

"What makes you think that?"

"Demographics," he said. "It's easy to manipulate the masses, play upon their ideologies, passions, and prejudices to sway their vote... but in the end, simple math will always win."

"I think you mean, almost always," Jack said.

Langhorne smiled. "I'd like to make you an offer," he said. "What kind of offer?"

"I'm starting up a new team for another project. I think you'd be a valuable addition."

"A job offer? You're kidding, right?"

"This one's secretly funded by a conservative think tank."

"You're switching sides?"

"There are no sides," Langhorne said. "Just those who have power, and those who want it."

Jack had assumed this whole struggle was about Democrats versus Republicans. Maybe he had been missing the larger picture. And maybe it was even uglier than he thought.

"Not interested," he said.

"Okay then." Langhorne stood to leave. "Good luck to you, Mister Patton."

"I hope you're not offended if I don't wish you the same," Jack said.

Langhorne smiled. "That righteous passion. You know, you could've gone far in this field." He slipped out into the crowd and was gone.

*   *   *

Vig and Miles had been trapped outside the main Capitol building during the commotion. They assumed at first that everyone was reacting to the shocking upset at the hands of the faithless electors. But soon enough, it became clear that their plan had failed.

Vig's hand was a mess; he got the pen out, but it had ruptured a vessel and wouldn't stop bleeding. He wrapped it tight, and also tied off his wrist to restrict the blood flow.

Vig got a call from Langhorne. It was just three words, but the meaning was clear: "Clean it up."

"What now?" Miles asked.

"We go back to the Nexus," Vig said, without looking up from his phone. "Shut it all down."

Miles glanced over at Vig's screen. It showed a GPS application.

"If we're going back, why do you need GPS?" Miles asked.

"We make one stop first," Vig said, and realized too late that Miles had already heard those exact words once before.

Vig grabbed him with his bad hand, but Miles broke free and started running. He ran north up Congress until it dead-ended at the University of Texas at Austin campus, and even though Vig had not pursued him on foot, he kept running north, past the Blanton Museum and toward the on-campus housing. He approached a Spanish-style building that looked to be a residence hall, but couldn't get inside without an ID card to unlock the door.

He kept moving, but at a brisk walk to avoid arousing suspicion. At the next entrance to the dorm, a student held the door open as he shouted something to a friend across the street. Miles slipped past the student with a nod and went inside.

The laundry center was vacant, save for one girl who was preoccupied with a statistics textbook. He walked to the opposite side, out of her sight. Several dryer units were tumbling loads of clothing. The second unit he opened had dry clothes that fit him well enough.

The bathroom was communal, but Miles had it to himself for the moment. He dug through the trash and found a discarded disposable razor. He pumped a handful of liquid soap into his free hand, then chose the last toilet stall on the end and locked himself in. He knelt in front of the bowl, took a deep breath, and dunked his head in. Once his hair was fully soaked, he rubbed the liquid soap into his scalp and went to work with the razor.

Shaving his head took longer than expected, but the end result was worthwhile: he was almost unrecognizable. He ditched his old clothes in the bathroom trash can, then headed toward an exit on the opposite side of the building from where he entered. As he passed through a large study area, he spotted an unattended backpack and snagged it without missing a step.

Outside, in his new clothes and new haircut, Miles walked toward the heart of a campus that boasted fifty thousand students, and disappeared.

49

"I LOST DAD'S PEN," Jack said.

He and Vera Lynn were sitting on the grass next to their father's grave on Marbletop Hill. It was Christmas Day, and the wind from the north was just cold enough to make Jack wish he'd worn a jacket. It didn't look like rain, but there was a steady rumble of thunder—like a stampede of wild horses—somewhere just past the horizon.

"I'll think he'll forgive you," Vera Lynn said.

"I also wrecked one of his suits."

"I don't imagine he'll be needing it any time soon."

They sat in silence, until Vera Lynn suddenly started laughing to herself. "I was just thinking about that guy in the barn," she said, "when the bugs went down his shirt. The way he jumped around, shouting."

"Yeah, it was pretty hilarious," Jack said. "Up until the almost dying part. How's Waylon, anyway?"

"Still at the house," she said. "He ain't convinced yet that those folks won't come back."

"Can't blame him," Jack said.

"I helped him get a job at the Senior Center."

"Sounds like you're good for each other."

Long pause. "We're not dating," Vera Lynn said.

"I never said you were."

"Good."

Jack's bandaged foot was starting to throb, so he switched positions.

"Your friend up and walking yet?" Vera Lynn asked.

"Silas? Yeah, he's getting by on crutches. And the management company at that building where he got hurt? They're desperate to settle with him. Ready to give him a pretty big chunk of cash just to keep quiet. Can you believe that?"

"But it wasn't their fault he got attacked," she said.

"I've stopped trying to make sense of things," he said.

Vera Lynn just shook her head and stared off at the horizon. "You know... this thing you did. Daddy would be proud."

Jack's throat clenched up, and all he could do was nod. When he was finally able to speak again, he said, "Dad almost had it right."

"What's that?"

"The potential for greatness that he saw in me. He was close. I just think he picked the wrong kid."

Vera Lynn scoffed and waved him off.

"Vera Lynn... I think you should run for office."

She laughed, and it was the kind of unguarded, full-bodied laugh he hadn't heard from her in years.

"Seriously," he said. "I think you'd be the perfect person

to look after this town. And we need more people like you representing the rest of us."

"Yeah right," she said. But she looked off at the horizon again, considering it. "I might could try for city council, if that'd make you happy."

Jack smiled. "But you know, you didn't do yourself any favors by giving away one of your best stories."

"What're you talking about?"

"You know full well," he said. "The tornado. Mrs. Wiegert. It wasn't me that went and got her. It was you."

She shot him a sly glance. "That ain't the way I remember it," she said. "And besides, Daddy's gone, Mrs. Wiegert's gone... who do you think people around here are gonna believe?"

"Not even in office yet, and you're already lying like a politician." Jack put his arm around her and pulled her close, kissing her on the forehead. He stood up, brushed the grass from his pants, and reached into his pocket.

He pulled out a single folded sheet of paper: his unused elector ballot.

"Sorry you never got to cast your vote," Vera Lynn said. "Kind of a shame, since that's what this whole mess was about."

"Not really," Jack said. He placed the unused ballot on his father's grave, and put a stone on top to hold it in place.

50

"THAT'S IT FOR MY STUFF," Marlene said, sliding a lid onto the copy-paper box on her desk. The entire place, aside from Jack's office, was emptied and broken down into its component parts.

"Need any help with it?" asked Silas.

"It's a box," Marlene said.

"I'll carry it out for you," he said.

As they walked out, a package delivery man asked them to hold the door. He wheeled in a large wooden crate.

"Whoa," said Jack. "Are you looking for the frozen yogurt shop? That's next door."

The delivery man checked his handheld scanner. "Jack Patton. Roundabout Design. That you?"

Jack nodded.

"You're over twenty-one, I assume?" He handed Jack the scanner and tapped on a signature box. "Just need to make sure, since it's alcohol."

Jack signed for the crate and looked around for a screwdriver to pry it open. Why on earth would someone be sending him alcohol? Was someone pouring salt in his wounds, celebrating the fact that his business was closing?

Langhorne had said Jack would be left alone, but he couldn't shake the feeling that his life was still besieged by invisible enemies, gnawing away at his resolve from all sides. Perhaps that was just the kind of paranoia he was cursed to live with after foiling a grand-scale conspiracy.

Either way, things had never recovered after the election. The property manager's lawsuit against him was ultimately thrown out, but only after Jack spent thousands of dollars in legal fees. In hindsight, he could have saved the money and done all the work himself, if only he'd known where to start.

And the business clients stopped coming, even after Jack got the false online reviews removed. He couldn't help but wonder if that was all his own fault; ever since the elector debacle, he had been suspicious of anyone that walked through his door. He questioned everything, and avoided any potential clients that gave him an uneasy feeling in his gut. Marlene pointed out to him more than once that his gut didn't seem to like anyone, and business was suffering for it.

But at least she was landing on her feet. She had parlayed her work experience into a junior designer position at an up-and-coming firm downtown. It was the kind of opportunity Jack would never have been able to offer her himself.

Silas would be fine too, when his injury settlement came through. He had pledged to give most of it to Jack to keep the business running, but he wasn't sure when the money would start rolling in, and Jack flat-out refused to accept it anyway.

Silas and Marlene came back in. Noting the crate, Silas said, "You're doing it wrong, buddy. We're supposed to be emptying this place out, not filling it back up."

"Anybody remember which box the tool kit is in?" Jack asked.

Marlene went straight to the correct box and opened it. Jack pulled out a flathead screwdriver and pried the lid off the crate. Between layers of padding sat six oak boxes with golden hinges and latches. Jack pulled one out and opened it. Inside, resting gently in a steely blue satin lining, was a bottle of Mount Gay 1703 Old Cask Selection rum from Barbados.

"Wow," Silas said. "That's some fancy stuff. Who's it from?"

"I have no idea," said Jack. "But take a bottle and enjoy it." He closed the oak box and handed it to Silas, and pulled out another for Marlene.

"There's an envelope in this one," Marlene said after she opened hers. The outside of the envelope said simply, "Jack." He opened it, unfolding the sheets carefully.

It took several seconds for his brain to process what he was seeing. The first sheet was a note, written with a delicate and elegant hand, that read:

Decency should be rewarded.

—*C*

The second sheet appeared to be an account statement from the First Royal Bank of Anguilla. As far as Jack could tell, the account was opened in his name. Hand-written in the margin, it said: "Pin #: 270." And at the bottom was printed:

ACCOUNT BALANCE: $1,000,000.00

Paper-clipped to the back of the account statement was

a plane ticket. First Class, Austin to Anguilla, by way of San Juan, Puerto Rico. Departure date: tomorrow.

"What's it say?" Marlene asked.

Jack's mind raced. Was this real? As skeptical as he had become, everything about it seemed genuine. He knew there was money set aside for the faithless electors... he saw at least some of it with his own eyes. Maybe Candace robbed them blind when she left. Good for her, he thought. And, apparently, good for him too.

With that kind of money, Roundabout Design could be saved. They could unpack everything and pretend the bad times never happened. Or even better, they could upgrade to a real office suite where hazardous medical waste didn't drip from the ceiling. Things could be the way he'd always imagined before real-world limitations forced him to simply make do.

But as he opened his mouth to tell Marlene and Silas the good news, something pinched in the back of his throat. He could save the business.

But should he?

Marlene already had a better job, and Silas could kick around for quite a while before he'd have to think about earning a living. Maybe it was time for them to move on. They'd always be friends, but that didn't require them to sit next to each other eight hours a day, five days a week.

And what about him? He hadn't been at his best—creatively or professionally—for months. He felt like he needed to reboot his life somehow, make a drastic change that set him on an entirely different course. He had actually been toying with the idea of going back to law school. Somewhere up there, he knew his dad would get a kick out of that.

But maybe he needed a break first. A trip would be nice, and with the brief but nasty Texas winter upon them, now was the perfect time to get away.

"Jack?" Marlene said.

"Huh?"

"Who's the note from? Is it somebody you know?"

"Not really," he said, and tucked the envelope into his pocket. But maybe, he thought.

Maybe that could change.

For the first time in a long time, Jack found himself looking forward to tomorrow.

"The greatness of America lies not in being more enlightened than any other nation, but rather in her ability to repair her faults."

—Alexis de Tocqueville, *Democracy in America* (1840)

19671927R00172

Printed in Great Britain
by Amazon